I0769513

the GREEN FORTY

BOOK ONE: RESCUE

CHRISTOPHER PAUL WHITE

"…A certain man had two sons."
—Luke 15.11

The author's granddad was a heavy machine gunner in WWII, a German POW
for 19 months, and a real man.

This book is dedicated to him.

Part 1: Granddad

Chapter 1

May, 1987—near Culleoka, Tennessee

Malachi

I once believed that the Alice Benjamin part of my story was meant for me alone, at least before Jonathan came to the Forty.

But it turned out I was waiting for a moment.

And so was he.

But I'm getting ahead of myself.

I haven't grasped the hand of a living man in too long. Everybody's chasing money. Or things. Or money *and* things.

But back in 1924—when I was twelve—the world was still real.

You could touch the living, and they touched you back. People were substantial; we all worked hard, and together, we filled our bellies on the simple produce. It satisfied us.

But I aged, and the world died.

Perhaps it was dead already and I just became aware of it, but sometime between the end of the war and Woodstock, it happened: People stopped caring about the good of the nation, started going tribal, turned against their own families. I watched as most people regressed into primitive obsessions (money, things). Survival of the fittest, as if man were a beast. Or a machine.

But there were rare ones, different because they dared to actually live. It was like they owned the place but didn't need it. In so living, they became legend. They'd come from somewhere better and knew they were headed back soon. It was like they were gods, goddesses. Immortals.

Like Alice Benjamin.

Even now, in 1987, her memory is potent; intoxicating. She haunts me with the same power she held when we were but children together. She defied with the beauty of her life whatever was normal. Her essence was as untouchable as a windborne seed.

1

But wait a while: I was explaining why I hate the world and everything it stands for. Let me get back to that.

Used to be, when I made introductions with a stranger, I was greeted with a firm handshake. If that didn't happen, I knew better than to make friends from acquaintances because a man's greeting has always been a harbinger of his character.

But in 1987, I found insipid men everywhere.

Like Jonathan's father.

And in 1987, I trembled for what my grandson faced. There really is such a thing as evil, and its thirst for blood and fire is not quenchable. It'll get more than it can handle of both in the end.

Evil is both patient and subtle, so we the righteous must confront it, even when it is the accepted status quo in the world. I've taken enough knocks from that old bitch to see through her mask and behold her as she really is.

She's an ancient grimalkin, a devil looking for a soul, and she hates old men like me because we have discovered she's a liar and publish the news to anyone who'll listen. Therefore she harries us and schemes to hasten our deaths; indeed rendering some dead even while they draw breath.

She succeeds with far too many.

Now that I can look over my shoulder at more than seven decades, I can see things pretty clear and straight, if you ask me. It's just enough time to make a man feel—well, not too old, that's not it. Tricked, maybe. Cheated. Like something's been stolen.

To tell the truth though, seven decades is but a moment, and I'm not complaining. People misunderstand old men.

What I'm saying is we were made for more. And if I weren't so timeworn, I'd ask for another chance, knowing what I know. Trouble is, knowing what I know, I'd be a fool to ask.

That's the thing. Man coined words like paradox to try to put deep questions to bed, but it is a proven fact that we know precisely the square root of jack diddly about the most important things. Calling the status quo a paradox doesn't provide satisfaction, does it?

But yeah. It's the best we can do when we swerve into God's territory. We should have surrendered that stuff to Him a long time ago.

And some of us might honestly have tried, if only for a season or two. That's what religion says it does, but it lies. These days it's wearing a hat that says it's science, for God's sake.

But it's still the same old grimalkin, and we're still doomed to reappropriate paradox after tired paradox because we'd rather build a fence around an enigma than risk everything we *think* we own for the unvarnished truth.

And why? Because truth is one of the most painful things in the universe.

But in 1987, most men were either offended by such things or openly scoffed at them.

And that's why I trembled. Because I knew the world too well—and knew I'd soon depart it. Old men must either reckon with their mortality ahead of time or suffer mortal panic in the inevitable event—everyone does die. And everyone must enter the grave naked and alone.

But what would Jonathan do with the time that had been given him?

At some point, he'd have to stand on his own two feet and fight that ancient devil however it chose to show up in his life. Because whether he was ready or not, she was coming for him.

Chapter 2

Malachi

Late May meant mornings with the kitchen windows open—the cool, moist smell of shaded grass in the yard, the taste of Tang in a tall, thin glass stirred with a long spoon, the way the fine latticework of the screens smelled metallic in the Southern humidity.

My beloved Tennessee hills: verdant forest, fertile field, muddy river gliding cool over limestone and shale—home.

My grandson Jonathan and daughter Sarah came down on a long weekend to the Green Forty—the family homestead—all the way from Chicago.

Running from the Leonard, among other things.

So the Forty was Sanctuary on this late May day, and it was about time.

I stood on the front porch as Sarah's baby blue Ford Escort rolled from County Line Road up my quarter-mile gravel drive. I watched how her car raised an arrow of dust like the contrail of a jet.

Jonathan later told me the fields of young corn passing by his window for mile after mile on their trip were like a television set needing adjustment. The VH (Vertical Hold) knob on the back. Jonathan knew that.

Jonathan knew a lot.

He was twelve when he first came to the Forty.

They called Jonathan's father the Leonard. My daughter and grandson would never have used that moniker if he was within earshot, but as is the way with these things, it had spilled out one day and stuck as a code between the two of them. It simultaneously bonded mother and child together as it separated them from—and suppressed—this force of darkness, once invited into intimacy, now unmasked and kept at bay, known for what he really was.

He was several rungs below the scum of the earth, made worse because when he went away, he wouldn't stay away, damn him.

But my daughter was good to her only son, as she should have been. She hung in there when nobody else would, fighting for his life and future with the kind of I'm-putting-my-foot-down authority suggesting she saw the big picture.

But she knew when she needed help (when she was overmatched). She made me proud.

Jonathan couldn't get his mind around the big picture at age twelve, and thank God—most of the big picture would have been dark, ugly, and contingent upon chance (a small one at that) given the hand he'd been dealt.

Maybe he would one day learn to make peace with the trauma he'd suffered if he wanted to be free of it. But that's the kind of crap a therapist would have said. And I was pretty sure Jonathan had one, which I found made me sad. If only boys could talk things through with their fathers—God! What heroes could rise!

Sarah parked the car, and they got out.

She gave me a smile, and I saw hints of the goddess, Alice Benjamin, my Alice Benjamin, in that smile.

Jonathan wouldn't look me in the eyes.

She gave me a hug.

The boy showed me his back and pointed his nose out over the Forty as the sun sank down in the west.

"How was your trip?" I asked her.

"Long," she said. She was more tired than I'd ever seen her. "But good," and she flashed me the smile only a single mother uses.

I wanted to ask her what was wrong but didn't. I knew well enough. She would share what she was willing to share in her own time.

"Jonathan has done well this year," she said, trying to bring him into the conversation, her voice overloud. "Done with ninth grade at twelve years old and finishing early too; he's bright."

No response from the kid. Sarah sighed, puffing a stray lock of hair away from her eyes. I tugged on her ponytail a little, and she turned toward her daddy the way she always had.

She lowered her voice, and the boy shuffled away, hands in pockets, studying the gravel in the driveway. "I can't leave him a latchkey kid for the summer, Dad. I don't know if or when the Leonard might come crawling."

"I know, lovely." I knew the boy was nothing more than leverage for his father.

"I'm afraid, Daddy."

"And?"

She faced away and spoke in a quick hush. "It was one thing when he hurt me; I thought—I mean, I'm strong enough. I even forgave him for my ankle. But then he hurt Jonathan, and—" she stopped. "And that was the end. He put Jonathan in the hospital with two broken ribs. I thought if I made enough noise about it, I could scare him into leaving us alone."

"With what, cops and social workers?" This was the first I'd heard any of *this*. "When?" I clamped my lips down hard with my teeth.

"It was a couple months ago."

"What's his problem now?" I made fists. "He's back into drinking? Or drugs?"

She sighed. "It's not so simple, Dad. It's not predictable. I almost wish—"

"What is it, then?"

"He's just angry. That's all. Angry at the world for being here. And I need Jonathan to be safe."

I cursed. "I need you to be safe, Sarah."

"Oh, I am. Don't you worry about me. My daddy taught me how to use a weapon." She tried a smile on for size. It fit her, but it didn't fit the moment.

I cursed again. "Sarah. He knows where you live. I know how he is; he'll show up some night when you least expect it and try something terrible."

"No, he won't. I've got home security by Walther. And Smith & Wesson. And," she fished around in her bag, pulling out a slip of paper, "this is my new address. You're the first to know." She was radiant.

I let the scowl slip from my face. It took some effort. "Huh," was all I could say. "You did? All on your own? From Washington Heights to Oak Lawn?"

"Dad, I'm thirty-three. I'm all grown up. I have had the ability to do these things for some time now."

I pulled her into me and kissed the top of her head. "My lovely." I pulled back and searched her face. "You don't need anything?"

"Nope. So try to resist the idea of slipping cash into my purse when I'm not looking."

I pretended to be scandalized by this.

"It's a cute little bungalow in a neighborhood stuffed with sub-scribers to *Coot's Digest,* just like you." She smiled. She was adorable.

"So proud of my girl."

"Thanks, Daddy." She hugged me.

"You know," I said cautiously, "Oak Lawn isn't what it used to be."

She rolled her eyes, and I knew this part of the conversation was over.

So it was that Jonathan came to the Forty in late May.

At first the arrangement was for a couple of weeks. Sarah mentioned something to me about a summer camp in the area, some church or charity up in Columbia. She didn't want the kid to be a burden for me.

He was anything but.

Summer camp would never happen for him, and thank God. The boy needed so very much more than programs could ever provide.

Perhaps it's obvious he was homeschooled. Such things mattered to some people. Bigotry tends to need a lot of fuel. For people like my Sarah, homeschooling was the only option for her son in a world that was both hostile and dangerous, and most hostile and dangerous when cloaked in the garb of the professional, government-trained educator.

For a Green, though, what people thought about us and how we lived was none of our business.

Sarah and Jonathan came to the Forty desperate for peace.

I had a feeling it was going to be costly. But worth it.

She was too busy with career up in Chicago to hang around long, and I encouraged her to get a move on the next morning. I figured the boy and I might as well get started on growing him up, and we couldn't make any progress in that direction with Momma here.

Their early-morning goodbye the next day fested with the butterflies of disquiet. I could see it; it was all over them. They were standing at the edge of something.

But this was a good moment for the boy. He needed time away from his mother; he needed to get off the tit. Jonathan's life had encamped at a fork in the road. It wouldn't be too much longer before he decided on his own to pull up stakes and set off down one of them. And if something wasn't done soon, he'd likely choose the wrong one.

He was in mortal danger of growing up to become yet another boy in a man's body: needy, insecure, dead; a wraith of masculinity.

Like his father.

Something needed to be done because such a creature was not intended by God to walk the earth. A man is supposed to be a giver, and to do so, he needs to know strength like the back of his hand. He needs to know that leadership is not about power or privilege but service and sacrifice.

Jonathan needed that; he needed to come up against something bigger than himself, and that something, for once, needed to be benevolent.

He needed a good, long summer spent doing things a boy ought to be doing.

He needed to be somewhere the Leonard couldn't find him.

Somewhere Sarah could let go of him.

That's what parenting is: a steady letting go.

Chapter 3

Malachi

Next morning: "Are you finished with your cereal, boy?"

"Yes."

"Yes, sir."

Our eyes locked. "Yes, sir," he said.

There was fear in his eyes, which was good, but it was lit by something else—intelligence—which was better. It was the difference between a man content to learn obedience and a man capable of command, and Jonathan had that.

I wasn't sure what the Good Lord would do with it or precisely why He had placed it in him, but there was no denying its presence. There was only pulling the weeds out of it.

And since the boy's father was such a lowlife halfwit no-account piece of garbage who had left both him and my daughter alone (and left her alone too late), it fell to me, the only man in the boy's life, to try to bang some sense into his head.

"You miss your momma?"

He paused and thought about it. "Wouldn't you at my age?

"You sassin' me?"

"No, sir."

I grunted. I thought he was, but I hadn't come to breakfast for an argument; I had come to breakfast for breakfast. "We'll go ahead and do the dishes, since you're done eating." I got up and stepped to the sink, filling the left basin with soapy water and the right with fresh. "Wash, rinse, dry," I said, pointing out the assembly line layout.

He nodded and got to work.

"You like Tang?"

"Momma makes it; yeah. I mean, yes, sir."

Quick learner. "She got her taste for it from me."

"So, what are we doing today?" he asked.

I thought that to be both eager and earnest, and I decided I would like him for it. "You can come with me on my rounds again."

"Looking after the birds, Granddad—I mean, sir?"

"The morning chores this time, boy, but yeah. We have to check on the sow and the goat, too. Your momma give you chores?"

"Mm-hm. Yes, sir."

"What kind of chores?"

"I gotta clean up my room once a week. I dust and vacuum the house."

"Have to. Not gotta."

"Yes, sir. And I clean up after the dog."

I grunted. "I'll never understand why people want to bring an animal into the house." I waved my hands.

"Oh, the dog's alright. Mom needs her, I think. She gets lonely. I don't really care one way or the other, but I take care of her for Mom."

I handed him my dish so he could wash it. "You're a good boy, Jonathan." I meant it. I was glad they had left the stupid dog at home; I'd be too tempted to put the thing out of its misery.

Chapter 4

Malachi

Early the next morning, we walked the perimeter of the Forty so that Jonathan could familiarize himself with my boundaries. I looked after all forty acres, the homestead my great-grandfather had laid claim to many years ago. Both time and circumstance had favored the house of Green. The barbarism of civilization had kept its distance.

When I needed anything store-bought, I drove to Columbia. Or Lewisburg, if I had a wild hair. They were about equidistant from my place, but Columbia had a little more buzz about it; more going on. These trips were seldom necessary, though. Maybe once every couple of weeks I'd "go to town." More often, I found what I needed at the co-op in Culleoka, which was just up the road.

The boy and I walked the fenceline in the low but climbing sun. We could feel the clingy, cool remnant of night air recede as the warming of the light took up all slack and the day gained traction for movement. It was muggy already. There were still marshmallow islands of fog over the meadows in the low places.

I showed the boy how to check for rotten posts and broken wire and explained to him how a skim coat of rust on just about anything was alright. It meant a thing was being put to work, and that was good.

One thing I noticed right off—which I intended to remedy—was that the boy was entirely too clean. We therefore headed to the stable.

"Let's let the birds out," I said.

Jonathan ran on ahead, knowing what to do. He'd only been here one day, but he'd already taken notice of how things worked.

By the time I made it to the gate, he'd let them loose. Now there were a dozen hens underfoot, scurrying around in the high grass scratching for grubs and earwigs and seeds. The rooster strutted along behind his little harem. "Well, you ol' philanderer you," I said to him, "were you busy again last night?"

I caught Jonathan looking at me. He said nothing with his lips, but his eyes were quizzical.

"You know what 'rhetorical' means?"

"Yes, sir. It's a question that's too embarrassing for an answer."

I had to chuckle. "Good enough. Let's let the hog and the goat out, too."

We did, and the boy watched in what was either dumbstruck awe or stupefaction as the old sow ambled by. She must have been near six hundred pounds.

"So they just graze? You don't feed them otherwise?"

"No, not from spring to fall. The old sow gets some table scraps sometimes. But she likes the grass and the thicket over there." I pointed to the wild blackberry brambles growing in a tangle in the distance. "The berries fall off starting toward late summer, and she gobbles 'em like hog candy. Mushrooms, roots, walnuts. The goat, she goes for all that too, but she likes the prairie grass best. Makes her milk taste sweeter, and better for you, too."

Jonathan sidled up to the fence and rested his chin on his arms as he watched. I wondered what those eyes were causing that brain to think of.

Finally he said, "You don't name 'em?"

"Son, you don't name a thing that'll end up on your plate."

Having made sure the animals were tended to, that the henhouse and the stalls were clean, and that they had plenty of water for the day, we headed over toward the shop. The old Cadillac was in there waiting for a tire rotation and a tune-up.

I'd held off especially for the boy.

Chapter 5

Malachi

"You never met your Grandma Alice, did you."

Another rhetorical.

"This was her car." I walked around to the front. "Flick the switch over on the wall."

After finding it, he did, and the overhead fluorescents came on. It revealed the long, low shape of a 1939 Cadillac, a Series Sixty coupe dressed in black, sitting on wide whitewalls with red enamel wheels.

"Whoa," he said. He walked around it, keeping his distance, under its spell.

I watched in silence as he took in the shine of the louvers and bumpers, the black paint, the vee'd windshield, the long, wide, teardrop-shaped fenders, the low, complex curvature of the trunk lid, the eager forward slant of the B-pillars, the art deco Cadillac script at the rear, the upright grille in chromium at the front, and the goddess that graced the leading edge of the hood, leaning way out, pointing the way forward.

Finally, he rested: He took a stool by the workbench, leaning back on an elbow. He took off his ball cap and scratched at his head, reminding me of my father. For crying out loud, he reminded me of me.

"You noticed any girls in school yet?"

His eyes snapped to and locked on mine, and there was no pretense there. The spell was broken, but by the only thing right and proper that could have broken it. He said nothing.

"A wise man is slow to speak," I said, pausing. "I mean that as a compliment."

"I know." He looked me dead in the eyes, and it wasn't the self-knowing confidence of a boy becoming a man I saw therein but the fire of defiance in a scared child whose way might be lost, if only. A breeze would push him right over.

"Been out behind the shed after Sunday school, have we?"

He turned aside.

I chuckled. "But you ain't fiddled around like my rooster does," I laughed. "You don't know about all that yet."

He blushed as red as a strawberry.

I approached him. "But you know what beauty is. Don't you." I meant the car he'd been ogling; I was speaking figuratively (pretty much) and grasped him by the shoulder as I spoke. But he shocked me. Sobbing, he flung his arms around my waist and pulled us together, crying into my bibs for a good long while.

At first, I didn't know what to do. I hadn't had a child around in years. I had only ever raised his momma, and that pretty much flying solo. But I found my hands came around to cover his heaving shoulders, and I found my lips saying, "There, boy. It's alright. Granddad's here."

I had to pull one hand back to wipe at my own face, but mine were not tears of release. No, mine surfaced from the deeps of my soul, from a cauldron of fury, an insatiable hunger for justice and vengeance.

Why is it, I thought, *that we in this family are doomed to run the race alone?* I was ready to kill Jonathan's father on sight, good and slow. I wanted him to know what he was feeling and who had unleashed it upon him when it happened, and I wanted to make it linger before I released his eternal soul into the torment that patiently waited to claim him.

Chapter 6

Malachi

I showed the boy the star pattern of nut-tightening for the car's wheels, showed him how to use a floor jack, and showed him how, if he didn't have a second jack, to rotate the tires by using the spare tire to hold the car up.

I let him feel how delicate the plug wires were and how to keep them from seizing to the plugs by putting a dab of dielectric grease on the plug end before seating the wire boots over them.

He was fascinated that the grease didn't foul up conductivity.

Smart boy.

He felt the need to apologize to me for earlier, but I told him that family was the only place under the sun where nobody could escape from themselves. In other words, I understood perfectly. Love burns through the masks of pretenders but tests the genuineness of advocates until it gleams as gold. That's part of what family means, and testing proves things in the hope that value is realized.

His smile began to come back to him from wherever it had fled, and it wasn't too much longer before he told me he wanted to go see what the sow and the goat were doing.

I twisted his ball cap on his head and told him not to back any of them into a corner if he knew what was good for him. He grinned at me and said, "I'm not stupid, Granddad," and ran out of the shop before I could tell him to his face that "Nobody said you were, boy."

"Hey!" I called after him, "Whenever you get hungry, you can make your own sandwich at the house. Stuff's in the icebox. Wash up before and after."

"Yes, sir!" But he was already long gone.

I futzed in the shop for a while, as old men will do. Before long I got hungry myself and walked up toward the house.

My place was laid out centered on a low rise. On the south side of the hill—my backyard—a creek ran in the woods between me and the Munro place.

My father had built the little white stable with the cupola on the roof. It stood away to the southwest of the house, far enough away that it wasn't an offense, near-ish the hardwood forest that walled me in on all sides. On the other side of the backyard, on the southeast side, and closer to the house, was the shop and the '39.

A gravel drive ran under the oaks and sycamores all the way from County Line Road, to the north of me, for about a quarter mile. Then it ambled up a gentle rise toward the house, a typical nineteenth-century outfit in clapboard white with a front porch. The parlor and sitting rooms were up front, the kitchen and pantry were in back, and the bedrooms upstairs.

The carriage house, also white, I used for storage. It stood close by behind the house. I didn't have much reason to go in there until the boy came.

But I'm getting ahead of myself.

The outhouse still stood, but that was being generous and technical. I had filled in the hole in 1954, the year my daddy died. That was the year I moved back home to take care of the place. I had installed running water in the house immediately. Now, about thirty years later, the old outhouse had leaned in on itself, looking like a noose had been drawn around it by the eaves. "It's turned into a teepee," I said as I walked by. "Perfect project for a twelve-year-old boy."

Speaking of whom, I had no idea where he was. His momma would kill me if she knew that, but what did a woman know about raising a boy to become a man?

Fact was, the boy needed to be tested. And he needed to be allowed to test himself.

Women are nurturers; they understand the need for safety, not the need for danger.

If Jonathan didn't taste danger and testing that summer, odds were he would grow up in the image and likeness of his father. He'd be like most men: unable to give a woman what she needed—unable to give her what she really wanted.

In the final analysis, most men were just like the women who settled for them. No wonder the world was in such a state.

But by God, I wasn't going to abandon and abuse this boy the way his father had. I would make him *such* a thorn in the side of the respectable world.

It was best to let him go out and see what he could see, learn what he could learn. *I won't begin to worry until after sundown.* If the boy was that transported all day, I didn't want to be the one to bring the real world crashing back in on him before he was ready. There was more to life than the hands of the clock.

His momma may have known this, but she didn't understand it. Not like a boy would, and certainly not like a man would.

Men and women were different, and that wasn't just intentional, it was beneficial. The world didn't know—and couldn't begin to comprehend—treasures like this.

Chapter 7

Malachi

When I had finished my lunch and was headed back toward the shop, I noticed one of the doors to the carriage house had been slid aside.

It hadn't been opened in at least half a decade.

"Who's in there?" I knew perfectly well who was in there.

"It's Jonathan!" The boy was buried deep inside.

"I figured. Didn't you get any lunch? It's going on…three o'clock."

"I'm not hungry yet. Granddad, what's this?"

I peered into the dusty dark. The boy had found it irresistible to go snooping through the piles of old tools and parts and machines that I kept in the carriage house, and he had climbed all the way in over the piles to a hollow along the back wall. *Intrepid. Maybe even a little impudent.* I grunted. "Well now, wait a while. I can't see nothin'."

"Anything."

"What?"

"Can't see anything, Granddad. Sir."

I shook my head. "Boy knows it all, doesn't he. What've you got there?"

"It's a junky old bike."

"Junk!" Now I knew what he was holding onto. "That's Mud Cub One. My old bicycle."

He didn't say anything in response. I could tell that his gears were turning as he thought things over. "You rode this around as a kid?"

"Yeah. We didn't have all those different sizes and kinds like you kids have today. If you wanted a bicycle, there was one kind you got." I turned to go back toward the shop, toward my work.

"Mud Cub One?"

"Yeah, boy." I turned back toward him. "The legendary Mud Cub, the bike every boy my age had to have. Right there in your hot little hands is the first one they ever built. Serial number one."

"I've never heard of the Mud Cub before."

"Well. Neither had I when I first started working and saving my pennies. All I knew was I wanted a bike. But that was a full two years before I first laid eyes on him."

I paused, and the cynicism that attends age began stirring and flowing, bubbling up from the grave, pulling apart the dreamer in me by reason of all my unrealized expectations. I exhaled low and slow, turning away a little. "He's an old farm bike, Jonathan. You haven't heard of the Mud Cub because…nobody cares about him anymore."

"But I care about him. How'd you get the very first one?" The boy was looking at the bike now as if it were a superhero.

Which was what it was.

Once.

I closed my eyes and breathed in and out. *Why does he have to be curious about this story, of all of them? And all that comes with it?* "Don't you have a book to read or somethin'? When I was your age, we had to do summer book reports."

"No."

"Or I would go find a woods to explore, a creek to fish."

"I don't have a fishing pole."

When his eyes met mine, his reaction told me I was glaring, and I heard my daughter's voice nagging at me that I was being overharsh. I tipped my chin down and peered over my glasses. "You wanna hear the story?"

He nodded, his eyes wide, the saddle leaning against his waist, one hand on each grip of the bars. *Oh, my God.* I breathed in and out.

"Well, bring the old farm bike over here." I waded into the rust and dust and held a hand out. It took some strength, but he was able to lift the front wheel to the point where I could grab it. He fed the rest of it out to me as I began hauling it over and out. The boy followed along right behind it.

"The ol' Mud Cub," I said, bringing it out through the doors and setting it down on its rust-speckled wheels. "You ain't seen the light of day in…well now, wait a while…it must be at least thirty years."

Jonathan stood there, his feet on the ground again, looking antsy, winding up for the opening pitch. "That's the last time you rode it?"

"No. That's the last time the bicycle saw the light of day." I regarded the boy, and he regarded me. *Why is it that when I look at you, I can feel you sizing me up the same as I'm reckoning with you?* I leaned the handlebar toward his chest in a giving gesture. "Let's push him on down to the shop."

I didn't take my eyes from his, and he did the same. He was breathing like he was excited, and I could guess what he was thinking: *Will he let me ride it.*

It may not have been worded the same way, but then it didn't need words, did it? The language of men and boys is dark and mysterious. It often doesn't need words.

Chapter 8

Malachi

"Grab a seat." I kicked at a stool, sliding it partway out from under the bench, then flicked the switch on the work lamp. A yellow glowcone shot out and down from under its steel shade.

I moved toward the icebox. "Cream soda?"

"Yes, please."

Mud Cub One leaned up against the bench like a weapon. It was the steed of a gallant knight; everything about its shape spoke purpose, nobility, poise, and all of these as matters of fact. Even in its flat-tired state, assailed by years, it was almost a living thing.

The boy sat there staring at it, only glancing at the bottle when I handed it to him. "Bottle opener's on the bench leg," I said, demonstrating how with my own cream soda.

The boy did the same and took his first sip, licking his chops. "Granddad?"

"Yeah, boy. What's on your mind."

"Tell me stories."

This stopped me in my tracks. I wanted to leap for joy when he said these words. I wanted to dance; I nearly wept. The boy was starting to get it, and already.

In this moment, we two souls were living as the Good Lord intended. Just an old man with too many stories, and a young boy with too few.

This was the kind of thing that kept me hanging around.

Part 2: Jonathan

Chapter 9

Jonathan

Granddad looked at me a certain way, like he knew me—like he understood me. It was a thing I didn't realize I was missing until I saw it standing right in front of me.

So I dove for it: "Tell me stories."

I was starving to know—and to know more. I saw his eyes shine now, which helped me to believe in hope. Something deep within me came alive and danced.

"Well now, wait a while," he said. He said that a lot. "Let me think."

We sat in a pool of light at the tool bench, Mud Cub One leaning up against it like a soldier with one leg cocked. Maybe he'd bum a smoke or ogle a fine woman. Or both; there was no telling. The naked chrome lady on the prow of the Cadillac leaped for us. The sun came through the slats of the walls in blades, searchlights piercing through swirls of dust, striping the black Cadillac like a bee.

"First," Granddad said, "you need to understand something. The story I'm about to tell you isn't really about a bicycle. The Mud Cub plays his part in it, but the story's bigger than he is."

I looked at the bike for a minute and said nothing.

"It's a story about hard work. But mostly it's about love, Jonathan, and not the mushy kind. Did you know that a man can have feelings about a machine? Like this old Cadillac? Like the Mud Cub?"

Again, I didn't say anything. I waited. I wasn't fond of the feeling I got when I overspoke or spoke too soon.

"There's a satisfaction a man finds in precision. The way the gear change in the Cadillac slides home just so. The way the skip-tooth chain sounds on this old bicycle when you're pedaling as hard as you can and the wind is in your face at the top of a rise. A man can find harmony in the work of his hands. Do you know that?"

"I think I do, sir."

"You're going to. I will teach you."

I considered things. "Are you saying a man can fall in love with a machine, Granddad?"

"Not at all. A real man won't do that; he knows the reason he has feelings about a machine is because of what people have had to do with it. Do you want to be a real man?"

"Yes, sir." I said these words even though growing up was outside the boundaries of my understanding. I feared the unknown as much as Christopher Columbus' men had.

"Listen to me," Granddad said, "and I'll tell you something you need to know: your father is not a real man, Jonathan."

His voice was gentle, but the quiver in it betrayed something behind the veil. I knew rage well, but this version of it was somehow sober, which made it far more terrifying.

"Real men don't run away. Real men don't beat women and children. They won't hurt you—not on purpose."

I felt in my bones that he was right, but I grasped wildly, trying to hold fast to the only version of family I had ever known. It was undeniable that, as of this moment, it was imperfect and had issues, that it was beaten, tattered—even rotten. Still, I hoarded its shreds because it was mine.

Plus, it was all I knew.

"Real men walk steady, Jonathan. They know their own strength, but they use it well, to build and not tear down. You won't understand some of this yet, but you will as you make your own decisions. Let those decisions teach you. That's how life works." He paused and sat back, taking a sip from his soda. "The decisions you make matter."

But they never felt like they did. I never felt like *I* mattered, let alone my decisions.

I felt forgotten.

My thoughts washed out, flashing back to about a year ago, when I'd randomly seen the Leonard at the grocery store. I remembered well what had *not* happened, which made it more painful and reinforced my belief that I didn't matter.

He was by the ice cream, and I was eleven. Encountering him was the last thing I'd expected.

As I turned the corner into the aisle, I saw him and froze. I was Mowgli walking through deep jungle. The Leonard was my father, the man-king, but those black eyes didn't catch me. I fled on feet of silk, utterly noiseless.

Reaching safety a couple of aisles away, I found myself among thousands of bags of junk food, an earthquake rocking my head. *It's my own father; why should I run?* But I knew exactly why.

What kind of father provokes in his own boy an instinctual fear to run? But I knew exactly what kind.

Fact: the Leonard was unsafe.

I knew in the foundations of my heart that this was the exact opposite of what a father was supposed to be. Experience had taught me that sometimes lies masqueraded as truth. And when the mask came off, everything hurt.

I breathed. With each breath, my courage rose. I decided I would defy my doubt and fear: it couldn't be so bad.

So I turned around.

He would want to see his only son.

When I came to the ice cream aisle again, he was still there at the opposite end. He hadn't sensed me. He was deciding on an ice cream, which happened to be my mission too. I thought how cool it might be if we could maybe decide together.

And then what?

Maybe we would even pick the same kind. *But he likes rocky road, and I hate it.*

I made my way toward him. I pretended to shop for other things as I watched him from the corners of my eyes.

I got closer, my heart in my ears.

I was past the point of no return. I understood that this was going to hurt, and I believed as much, but I would happily pay the price for a chance to have a moment with my own father. Desperation stabbed, wastes poured in, and I gobbled all potentialities.

I could not run. Not if I wanted to.

He then decided: I didn't see what he chose, but he put a little tub in his basket and turned away, leaving me.

I stood alone as he disappeared.

And then it was as if he'd never been there. As if I had never been there. Never been born.

Except for the wake. *How can he not feel me?*

Other things had happened between then and now, including the one thing, about a month ago, that caused Mom to move us from Washington Heights to Oaklawn. He stormed into our house out of nowhere, drunk and raging. Mom and I both got hurt because he liked to throw punches at the people he said he loved.

I thought I believed his lies.

But when he randomly called a few days later, Mom was out, and I felt a weird hope about us. Any boy wanted an opportunity to know his father better.

So when he asked me what was new in my life, I told him what was up. We were moving soon. I didn't say where, but I did let it slip that I was headed to the Forty for a while.

It was about a month ago.

He'd only been to the Forty once—would he be able to find it? Would he even want to? It wasn't like I'd given him dates and an address, but he had a way. He found things out.

If he did come anyway, it couldn't be so bad. A father should want to see his only son.

Granddad would get that, wouldn't he?

But last time the Leonard and Momma had been in the same room, they fought like I'd never seen.

They fought over me, which made me feel like a piece of property.

It also made me feel like I had to choose between them, which felt wrong. It felt like my life was built on jello.

I had experienced consequence before: it was like standing under a landslide on purpose. And this wasn't something I would admit out loud, but I thought I could feel the earth beginning to tremble.

And if I knew any one thing, I knew this: if Granddad and the Leonard ever found themselves in a room together, somebody was going to die.

Chapter 10

Jonathan

Granddad had said, "The decisions you make matter," not even five seconds ago, and if that were true, I didn't like how it sounded. But I knew it was true. It had to be so.

Consequence.

Landslides.

"There is such a thing as treasure, Jonathan. I mean virtue, honor, innocence. These things are real, and you're going to have to fight for what you love. To guard your treasure, you are going to have to confront and defeat the dead men, I call 'em. Wraiths. Ghosts, like.

"They devour everything, they create nothing, and they won't leave you alone until you *make* 'em leave you alone. They can't understand honor or discipline or restraint. They only understand force, son."

I swallowed. *I shouldn't have told the Leonard I was coming here.* I wanted to confess everything I had done; I wanted to unload. "Granddad?"

"Yes."

I tried to think of a way to begin but couldn't. "Uh," I said, improvising, "what about the Mud Cub?"

"Oh. I am getting ahead of myself," he said, "you're right."

I breathed uneasily, having just purchased a patch in the garden of time for which I could see no price tag. Nevertheless, I also saw no way I could afford to pay up when the time came. But the commission and its moment passed. I felt like God was taking notes, and that felt sinister, which I knew was wrong. It just had to be.

"Mud Cub One here was my first bicycle," Granddad said. "I was ten years old when I bought him. Just a little younger than you."

I took a sip of cream soda and swallowed, clearing my throat. I was uncomfortable; I felt self-scrutinized and sweaty. But there was nowhere else I wanted to be than here, sitting on this stool with Granddad and Grandma Alice's '39 Cadillac and the Mud Cub. Therefore I listened like this story would save my life.

"The Mud Cub helped me woo your Grandma Alice."

I knew cognitively what the word woo meant, but I thought it sounded weird. I interjected. "So the Cadillac is hers, and the bicycle is yours?"

"Mm-hm. I bought him in 1922. The price was near fifteen dollars."

"What color was it?"

"Red, of course. You can't tell now, but it was bright red, fire engine red, and these yellowed lines along the curve of the top tube were pure white pinstripes, hand-brushed. Back then, that's how things were made; craftsmen had skill."

He ran a hand along the curve of the frame in a way that suggested affection but not love, though the gesture was familiar and held flourishes of both.

I realized then that the world contained mysteries I hadn't yet begun to imagine.

"Do you have any idea how much fifteen dollars was back then?" he asked.

"No, sir."

"Well, I'll tell you this: I remember, when I was ten years old, my daddy telling the pump attendant that the fact that gasoline was a whole quarter of a dollar per gallon was 'an outrage,' as he said it. Paying fifteen whole dollars for a bicycle was foolishness. Unintelligent. But boys are able to traffic in those things at that age and not suffer too much for it."

"How did you get so much money?"

"I earned it."

"How?"

"Didn't matter," he said, "I earned it." He took a sip. "I went out and did odd jobs around here. I asked the neighbors if they had things they needed done for which they were willing to pay me."

"Like what?"

"Well now, wait a while. I suppose I painted sheds. I dug outhouses and ditches. I mended fences. I milked cows and goats. Things like that."

"How long did it take you to save up for the Mud Cub? And how were you able to buy the very first one they ever made?"

"Hang on, boy, now *you're* getting ahead of me. Like a lot of things in life, it comes down to the people involved. And not only that but the timing. Timing means everything. You believe in destiny?"

I wasn't sure what to say, so I said, "I don't know, sir."

"Fine, fine. Don't answer." He waved his hands. He sometimes did that. "You're a shrewd one." He winked at me through his glasses and took another sip from his brown glass bottle.

"Let me tell you something, boy, it took me a long time to save up for the bike. A couple of long, hard summers working from sunup to sundown, lots of walking to and fro. I did a great deal of work over at the Munro place." He put all his weight into the first syllable, Mun-ro, as he pointed south through the shop wall toward the neighbors' family spread.

"But there were others, too. Like Mr. and Mrs. Benjamin, who lived the farthest out from me, but whom I saw often because of their daughter Alice."

"When did you meet her?"

"Hang on, boy. You're chomping at the bit. I know you need something to be excited about, but you need to learn self-control, too. Balance. Like riding a bike."

"Okay, well, how'd you get the bike?"

Granddad sighed. "After my tenth birthday—which is in July—my momma and daddy and I took a trip way up to Chicago. Back then, there was no Interstate Highway System. That came after the Second World War—Ike's brainchild. There were some highways, but they weren't the kind of roads you'd know. They were cinder or dirt in most cases.

"In twenty-two, way out here in the sticks, we had three realistic options for a long journey: take a horse, an automobile, or the train. Usually it would have been a combination of at least two of those, because the rail lines weren't right outside your door, you know, and the roads were usually so rough or muddy—depending on the weather—it was sometimes easier to ride horseback than it was to take a car."

I glanced at the Cadillac and tried to imagine a horse beside it.

"You've heard of Henry Ford's Tin Lizzie? The Model T?"

"No, sir." Where was he going with this? I didn't understand why he rambled off into stuff nobody cared about. "Do you have a picture I could look at?"

Granddad stopped. "Well now, wait a while. I suppose I do." He rummaged around on the bench until he found a greasy old shoebox, its cardboard looking more like leather. His weathered hands took the lid off, pushed some things aside, and finally picked out an old black and white photograph. He replaced the box on the tool bench.

I took the old photo and peered through it into the past.

"My dad had a Ford Model T," he said, his rough finger tapping the paper. The photo showed a man and a boy in what was basically the first car that mattered, the man behind the wheel, the boy standing on the wide running board with one leg up and in. I assumed the man was his dad, and the boy was Granddad. "Whoa."

"It was already near ten years old by then and didn't have windows on the doors, so the weather would get in and you'd get filthy. Even on Sundays. When you wore your best duds. For church."

"Did you guys take the car to Chicago?"

"No. Daddy got Mr. Munro's daddy to drive with us to the station in Nashville, where we got on the train." Granddad sounded serious.

"Why'd you and your dad go to Chicago? What was there?"

"The doctor. See, my momma was real sick. The local physician here, just a country doctor, told us there was nothing he could do for her and told us she needed a specialist in the city. He referred us to his mentor, a well-respected doctor in Oak Lawn up there near Chicago.

"The day after I turned ten, she fell ill. We were worried. Like I said, our local doc did the house call. He said we needed to make like the devil for Chicago. He put a slip of paper in Daddy's hand with an address and a telephone extension. He said he'd wire ahead for us and tell Dr. Stowe up there to be expecting us.

"About destiny, Jonathan: There will be times in your life when no matter what you do, you can't escape it." He locked eyes with me, pinning me in place with them. "And lots of times, boy, you have to take a little pain along with the good."

Chapter 11

Jonathan

"When we left here," Granddad said, "in my heart of hearts my world was at an end. I knew Momma was going to die. I didn't know if I would ever come home again, or if I could. The world had shifted, a change had occurred, and there was nothing I could do about it.

"I did the only thing I knew to do, Jonathan. I stuck my money in my pocket and took it along—just in case.

"I worried, selfishly, that maybe Daddy would need me to spend some or all of it on an emergency of some sort; maybe even on something to help Momma. That fifteen dollars and twenty-three cents was all I had in the world. Two years' wages.

"And I remember when, on the way to the station, I finally decided I would trade everything away if only I could do something to help her.

"But she died before we got there. That night on the train, Daddy took the floor, giving Momma and me the benches. When the sun began to overtake the darkness at the eastern edge of the world, I woke to a growing commotion. Daddy and some other men were trying to rouse her. I cannot forget how pale her face was, yet how peaceful, too. I knew as soon as I saw her that she was gone; she had not been able to hold on.

"It might sound strange, but my strongest feeling about it was peace. It wasn't the natural thing for me to feel, Jonathan. But I came to that peace by way of how my daddy demonstrated strength.

"I saw his shock. I saw the flash of his fear, and I would live with both his grief and mine for many years. But soon after the sun had risen, I heard in his voice what I needed to know. He wasn't giving up. He wasn't ignoring the problem. He was a man who wrestled with a God who knew more—and knew better than he did—why things happened."

I stood there looking in wonder at the Mud Cub and the Cadillac and my granddad. Old things and old men, I'd once thought, were relics waiting to be forgotten. But I could think that way no longer. Somehow, these old things and this old man were more than the sum of their parts. Granddad's life and times had been just as hard, even harder, than my own. And he'd come through. I couldn't explain it at twelve years old, but I starved for a heart so secure.

Granddad continued. "Daddy's steady voice was a soothing balm for the rest of our journey. He said to me, 'If the Good Lord saw fit to take her now, there's work yet here for you and me, and make no mistake.' I don't know if that gives you comfort, Jonathan, but it does me."

He was quiet for a moment. I didn't want to interrupt him. I didn't feel I needed to, and I sure didn't want to. I stared back and forth between the Mud Cub and the Cadillac, wondering what great stories underpinned them. Already the Mud Cub was becoming personal, more than machine, more like a family member.

After another sip of his cream soda, Granddad continued. "When we got to Chicago, the first thing we did was telephone Dr. Stowe. I don't remember much, but he took charge of the situation, and Momma was buried in the Oak Lawn cemetery by sundown the day after she'd died. The doctor made sure there was a minister on hand to perform the graveside."

He was quiet a while. Then I said, "What happened after that?"

Granddad nodded and took a deep breath. "Daddy and I put up in a boarding house, having already booked our return passage to Nashville and the Forty. He sent a telegram to the Munro house—" (again, he accented the first syllable) "—with the sad news and requested that they send someone to meet us at the station with the car. We were returning minus one soul."

I searched Granddad's face then, expecting grief. It was there but overshadowed by something bigger. Strength. And I wanted some for myself.

"We started the next day with a stroll," he said. "We visited Momma's grave, where we both wept on our knees. We each placed a single carnation on her modest plinth there, then we walked away. It was what we could do, and it wasn't much. But I came to peace with the fact— years ago—that it will never feel like enough. We did what we could.

"We had some time to kill. Our train didn't leave until late that night, so we kicked the can and beat feet through the village. Oak Lawn wasn't very big back then, but there was a Ford agent—that's what they called car dealerships—on one of the busy corners, and on another corner, there was a bicycle shop. I gravitated toward it."

I sat forward on my stool, my cream soda forgotten on the bench as I gazed at the rusty old bicycle.

"As I was looking in through the shop window, I saw the Mud Cub." He gestured toward the bike like it was a colleague. "There he was, right in the middle of the shop before God and everyone, like he owned the place."

"And you bought it then?"

Granddad nodded. "As soon as I saw him, it started to rain."

Chapter 12

Jonathan

I realized I still held the photograph of the Model T in my hands. The automobile was their fortress, and the man and the boy looked right back at me, audacious, right through the lens. Through all those decades.

I turned the photo over and read two names and a date. The reverse image bled back through, carried on the light. Over the boy's face in an old-fashioned sweeping scroll was the word Malachi.

His dad's name was Albin.

The date recorded was 1921.

Below it, someone had titled the photo "Two Warriors."

I wondered offhand who had written it and who had been behind the camera.

"Was it your momma?"

"Hm?"

"Who took the photo, your momma?"

"Yes. She would have had…wait a while…I guess she had less than a year to live when this was taken."

"She took the time to do it?" I held it up, wondering if it was possible for people who were going to die soon to work a camera. "This was for you, wasn't it, Granddad? The title and everything."

"Yes." He took his glasses from their perch and began cleaning the lenses with a cloth he kept in his breast pocket. "It means a great deal even now that she titled it thus."

"Two warriors," I said. *Oh my God,* I thought. How I starved for that kind of identity for myself, and I never knew how bad I'd needed it until the moment I saw their faces and those words.

I flipped the photo back over to reckon with the eyes of my ancestors, to see what clues to the riddle of life might lie therein.

I wanted to be brave, too.

I wanted to have a face like flint, to be invincible.

"Mother. Wife," he said. "Each one a one and only. You'll only have one mother, and if you do it the way I did, you'll only ever be the husband of one wife."

I soaked myself in the steely shades of the image, taking in the lay of the blades of grass, the old Ford's burnished brass radiator and dirty black paint, the fresh, whitewashed house in the background, and the yearling green of trees then small, all of it rendered in grays that prophesied of colors that could well be imagined, at least for me. These same sycamores had grown to become giants, now spreading gorgeous shade and sheltering the edges of the Forty beneath their broad canopy. It was mind-bending.

If trees could speak, would they tell stories of the time march? I was sure they had something to say. I believed if anyone knew their language, they could communicate to me what the man and the boy would say to me. I longed for ears that could hear these whispers in translation.

I could be friends with the boy in this photo; we could play a game of catch together. He would be black and white, and I would be Kodachrome, but we could hang out.

I ached even to be near what he had: a good man. That didn't mean I loved my momma any less. The photograph was, for me, hard evidence that, no matter how she tried, there was no way she could give me what I saw here.

The plain realness of the man, the ambitious-almost-savage boy at his side, how they stood, brazen and unapologetic, shoulders-across at the camera lens, squared up against the whole world.

It meant they were inseparable.

They looked through time as if they dared somebody to be witness to their legend on a coming day so many years from the one pictured.

The comfortableness inherent in their relationship was plainly stated without words in their posture: they counted on each other. They were family through everything, through whatever test would come. That man would never walk away from that boy.

That hurt me deep, *so* deep. And a tear dripped from my cheek onto the photograph. I didn't have the courage to say so, but I needed my granddad more than I wanted my next breath.

I was desperate, lost at sea the same as if I were one of Morgan's shanghaied deckhands, and I'd been caught not by a Caribbean storm but a storm of a different kind. Shipwreck threatened.

I was going down.

Granddad was dry land.

I breathed in spasms now, turning toward the '39 once more. I put the photo down on the bench and got up, walking along the driver's side of the long, low, curvaceous shape. Granddad said nothing for a good long time. My heaves soon calmed; my breathing again moved to the back of my mind.

"Well, Charley," he said (he called me that sometimes), "we ought to get you some supper. It's a little early, but you missed lunch. You could use some meat and potatoes." He stood and walked toward me, placing a hand on my head and messing my hair up, sticking my ball cap back on when he was finished.

Momma never said she loved me this way.

"We need to get you some bibs like me," he said, his thumbs pulling against the shoulder straps of his overalls. "You'd want that?"

"Yes, sir," I said.

"Good boy," he said. "Let's go eat. Tomorrow, we'll head to the co-op after we go fishing."

Chapter 13

Jonathan

When Granddad woke me the next morning, the sun wasn't even considering our side of the world.

"Wake up, Jonathan. I've got breakfast. Then I'll need you to help me get the boat hitched."

I wasn't half aware of anything by the time he'd walked out of my bedroom, but I sat up and got up in spite of myself. I was afraid of what he might do if I fell back asleep and made us late.

My fresh eggs woke me further, as did the bright taste of Tang in my glass. We made a plain lunch of peanut butter sandwiches, packing each a can of Royal Crown Cola and a little yellow bag of Lay's.

"Let's go get hitched, else the fish will wake up and eat their breakfast before we can offer them our minnows. If it goes well, we'll be frying up some crappie and smallmouth for supper tonight. Maybe even catfish."

Outside, I stumbled through the hand signals he showed me. Eventually, in spite of my helpful guidance, he'd backed the Chevy—not the Cadillac—to the boat. As he hitched it up, I felt how cool and quiet everything was, and I couldn't believe how dark the sky could be and still be blue and not black.

The stars gleamed as distant worlds, and I was on the flight deck of the *Millennium Falcon*, firewalling the throttle, blurring bright worlds into streaks.

Granddad's Chevy (a model named the Celebrity, as ubiquitous as dirt in 1987) towed his aluminum boat on its lightweight trailer behind us, tossing side to side, the trailer yanking the car back to front over the frost-heaved and potholed, shoulderless county roads.

We bought nightcrawlers and minnows at the bait shop, and Granddad told the clerk to throw in a pouch of Red Man.

I didn't know how it was possible for chewing tobacco to smell like raisins, but it sure did.

The clerk said to me, "Don't tell Gray-Maw," with a wink. Granddad shot back, "Ol' Gray-Maw's dead, and what she don't know ain't gonna bother her where she is no how," and they chuckled between each other as older men do.

Granddad bought me a pouch of Big League Chew bubblegum so each of us could have something to dip finger and thumb into.

Then we headed to the river: the mighty, muddy Duck.

The sun wasn't up yet, but the eastern horizon was struck with a wide brushstroke of aquamarine singed with black-orange fire at the edge of the earth.

Granddad unplugged the trailer's lights, unhooked the rear of the boat from the trailer on both sides, and backed the rig down the launch in a single shot.

"Grab this," he said, handing me a rope that was fastened to the bow. I walked a floating dog; I had a boat on a leash. "Don't lose that, boy, or you're swimming to go get it." He drove up and out, wrenching the bare trailer from the depths, great clear-green sheets of river water rolling and rising, then cascading in falls and leaving a shimmering path all the way over to the little gravel parking area.

I stood on the dock staring at the boat, at the engine, sensing speed and danger and potential.

It was chilly out, but it would get hot quick.

"Alright, Charley," he said. "Put this in there." He handed me the green steel cooler, relieving me of boat-leash duty. He pulled the boat closer and steadied it. "Step over the gunwale into the middle of the boat and try not to fall in."

I did so, nervous but determined, beholding the rivets in the aluminum and the small puddle of water inside the boat back by the engine.

"Sit up here by the bow." He motioned to the forward seat. "Flip the backrest up and—there you go." He climbed aboard, and the boat leaned so much I threw my arms out for a moment to balance.

But the seat I was in swiveled. *Nice.*

I turned to see him fiddling with the cooler and the tackle box, then yanking on the engine's pull cord. As he did all this, we drifted out away from the dock, the boat pulling away at an angle. Then finally the motor brapped to life in a cloud of blue-gray smoke. It tasted sweet and dark when it mixed with the moss and mud of the Duck.

We turned pretty quick, heading upriver, and the bow rose out of the water in response to the rise of the engine's one-note song.

Granddad didn't have to tell me to hold on.

I rode the nose of a dolphin or piloted a low airplane; I wanted to hold my hands out wide, palms down, and make like I was flying—but I didn't.

I could smell the water.

The trees on the banks were crumples of construction paper in predawn's mysterious shades.

Granddad throttled back after a while, and the bow came down. As our wake overtook us, the boat surged from back to front.

I was alarmed at first; the motion was unfamiliar.

I heard a *plish*. Granddad had plunged the electric trolling motor into the water. I listened to the quiet hum it made as we turned and drew in toward an eddy near the shore. A grove of trees and scrub drooped their branches low over the water.

"Be quiet, Jonathan. Remember, you can scare the fish off if you're too loud."

"Yes, sir," I whispered.

"Let's get them fish poles." They rode pinned to the inside surface of the hull under catches made of wood. Granddad had made those catches; they couldn't have been bought anywhere. One twist and the pole was free.

The anchor made not a sound when Granddad lowered it, and the boat came to a gentle swinging stop. We hovered in the mild current over the shallows. The river was slow here.

"We're gonna cast over there," he whispered, pointing toward the water in the hollow where the trees drooped. "There's a mess of catfish in there, I bet. I'll set you up on a bobber for smallmouth, and I'll set me up for fishing cats off the bottom.

"Set your pole down in the boat like this," he said, showing me how to grasp the rod and let the handle rest down in the hull. "You're gonna use the minnows."

He fished one out of the bait cooler with a little green net and offered the wild little flipping creature up to my hand. "Grab him and hook him right under his dorsal fin. The one on his back."

I grasped the minnow so hard I had killed it by the time I'd hooked it. It was wiggly; I had to hold on hard.

I did this with the next one, too. I had killed two living things.

Meanwhile, Granddad's hook and line had been in the water for five minutes already.

"Let me see him," he said, minnow-baiting my hook in two seconds, then handing the rig to me. "Cast over your right shoulder, a little to the side like this," he made the motions, "and remember I'm sitting back here, and you'd better not hook me." He wagged a cautionary finger.

My first cast put the whole shebang right into the trees.

Chapter 14

At length we achieved a state of calm nothing, a kind of boredom by a different name so it sounded better.

I wondered if it was a good time to ask Granddad to continue the story about the Mud Cub or about Alice, but part of me thought it was a bad idea to speak at all on the boat.

He had already shushed me twice.

Our lines were in the water, everything around was even and quiet and still, the sun having risen bright and already warm. The bottom curve of its gold disc shimmered close by the tops of the trees in the river cut.

We watched the steady flow of the river's surface, my bobber making lazy ripples in response to whatever creatures down there were cruising by or checking on the temptation we'd laid out for them—the one with the wicked barbed surprise inside it.

But there was action soon enough. I hauled in two fish as big as my forearm by lunch, and Granddad had gotten a couple of cats and some crappie. There was more than enough to feed both of us for days. My mouth watered thinking of it—the crisp breading and skin, the white flake of meat on my fork.

We strung our fish through the gills, me being careful to keep away from the whiskers of the cats, since he'd told me they could sting.

By ten o'clock we'd eaten our sandwiches and chips in total silence and had caught our limit, so we hauled in the gear.

Our catch moved in and took over the green metal cooler, along with a big dose of cool river water he bailed in.

The motor barked, and we plowed back downriver to the boat launch, where I watched and stayed out of his way as he shifted the boat from wet and alive to dry stasis.

The man amazed me.

I stood and observed as he went about his business, taking mental notes on how he did everything. I reserved my questions for when we were back in the Chevy and headed to town.

"Why do you unplug the lights?"

"They'd blow if I left them plugged in. They're not waterproof, and water and electricity don't mix."

"What would happen if you forgot?"

"The worst would probably be a blown fuse. The fuse box is behind this panel." He pointed toward the dash by his knee.

"What's a fuse do?"

This went on all the way to Culleoka.

It was an average little village, with a main street consisting of a twenty-five-mile-an-hour speed zone and a few buildings crowding up against the county road, and the closest thing to civilization anywhere near the Forty. The center of activity was the co-op, nestled in a slice-of-pie angle between the road and the tracks.

The railroad ran along on top of an arrow-straight wall of earth dressed out in chipped gray rock standing about ten feet higher than the county road in some places.

Grain silos made of concrete towered over us at least five stories into the sky. We walked in their stony shadows toward a low tin-roofed building with a sign over the door that read CO-OP in red, white, and blue.

There was a service counter inside where a few leathery old toughs depleted of all mirth stood around waiting on whatever they were waiting on. I was ignored by them. The wooden Indian statue by the door seemed more lively. And interested.

"Afternoon, Malachi." A man with yellow eyes stood behind the counter. A big brown bruise had spread on the Formica right in front of him where the material had been worn. There were shelves of catalogs behind him, calendars with tractors on them, and a green and yellow tractor-themed clock on the wall.

"Afternoon, Bud." Granddad introduced me to Bud, who nodded but regarded me with what I could only interpret as either suspicion or irritation.

Granddad told him I needed a set of bibs, whereupon he harrumphed and began flipping through papers on his clipboard and looking through his catalogs. The ringing of the telephone on the wall interrupted him once, but after that, he disappeared through the greasy double doors behind the counter to "go have a look-see."

We walked out of there with a brand new set of dark blue bib overalls a little too big for me. Granddad said I needed room to grow, and I didn't complain. I would roll up the cuffs like Momma had taught me, for when my britches were too big.

We checked on the fish. They were still cool and swimming.

So we headed home to gut them.

Chapter 15

Jonathan

Out back of the shop at a stainless steel sink under a lean-to roof, Granddad showed me how to kill the fish by clubbing them to death with the big end of a twelve-inch Crescent wrench. The fish were held down by the tail in turns on a thick wooden clipboard with a jagtoothed spring clamp at its top edge.

The bass and crappie didn't take much, but the cats were tough. I hit them as hard as I could several times, but they still wriggled. Granddad had to finish those.

"So, the Mud Cub," he said, picking right up where he'd left off the day before. "When I saw it," he picked up a knife with a long, thin, curved blade, "I knew it could be mine. The only question was whether I would choose to pay the price and take it home with me.

"Of course," he said, opening up a crappie's belly from its tail to its jaw, "there was the problem of my father's say-so. The Mud Cub was the brave new language of manhood, and I trusted that my father would not only understand my need for it but also perceive how time was of the essence, given we had just buried Momma."

He cut off the head, pulled the innards out with two fingers, and dropped them into a bucket.

"Is it for the sow?" I asked.

"Nah, these guts will go into the compost. Anyway, all this about manhood—I knew it in my gut, not in my head. As I mentioned, it started raining, so we opened the door to the shop and went inside.

"Now, this felt like destiny—the rain coming up right when it did— and I intended to take full advantage of it. The details about getting the bicycle home on the train with us, of getting it home with the car from Nashville, were about as far from my mind as possible."

He took up a jagged tool and began raking it against the sides of the fish, working from tail to head, popping the scales off. Some of them stuck to the tool, and some were flung all over the place. His forearms got plastered with the fishy little silver currency as he worked.

He took up the next fish and continued. "See, you work him like this," he said, opening the belly of a smallmouth bass and gutting it in a few expert flicks of the blade, cutting the fins off, too.

"Now, you scale him." He handed me the scaling tool.

As I took it, my stomach seized.

The wood handle was sticky.

The smell of fish was strong.

I wasn't sure if I was hungry for fish fry at supper anymore. I'd never done this kind of thing in my life. I had killed the minnows and tried to kill the catfish I'd caught. I wasn't too sure how I felt about that either, seeing them dead on a plank.

One at a time, though, we would convert them from living creatures to food.

My hands were unsteady as I tried working the scaling tool for the first time in my life. The amount of force it took to remove a fish's scales from its skin surprised me. Soon my own forearms were peppered with silvery dots too.

Granddad began working on the catfish with the knife. "These don't have scales, so you gotta pull the whole skin off." He went to work with a pair of needle-nose pliers.

The fish heads, the skin and scales, the fins, and the guts went into the bucket.

I could hear the sow around the corner snuffling nearer, her vanguard of hens clucking around her.

Granddad continued. "When we closed the door of the bicycle shop behind us, I was aware there were at least a dozen other bikes standing on the floor, but I didn't need to look around. The Mud Cub was under a light up on a plinth, and it sang me a siren song. You know about the sirens?"

"No, sir." I was still working on scaling the first smallmouth bass and eyeing the next one with something like regret that slowly churned and stiffened into revulsion.

"Greek mythology. They were these beautiful naked women who would sing sailors to their deaths on the rocks." Granddad's eyes were hooded under his white brows as he checked his glance down at me. "There is such a thing as an unbeautiful naked woman, too. That's why I say that."

"Huh?"

"Yeah. That'd be any naked woman other than your wife, Jonathan, whether she's naked for real or naked in your head. But wait a while; where was I?

"Oh, yeah. Sirens. Sirens are dangerous. And I might warn you to be careful in life, but there are times when careful's dangerous too."

"Careful's dangerous?"

"It is when you confuse it with fear. Fear takes things from you. Opportunity, like. There are times when you have to leap into danger, son." He waved the knife around, looking a little dangerous himself. "Or uncertainty."

I felt sick and wasn't sure if it was the fish or the conversation.

"Beautiful and unbeautiful," I whispered. Then I asked, "How do I know the difference?"

"Faith is wholesome and pure, Jonathan, and it usually—not always but usually—has more to do with what we're going to be able to do for others than it does with us. At your age, though," he said, turning back to skinning the cat with the pliers, "I wouldn't worry much about it."

My hands moved irresolute over my fish, and the tool tore through the skin into the meat.

"I'd seen him in comic books," he continued. "Heard about him on my favorite radio shows. I dreamed the Mud Cub could do anything. I believed I could swing a leg over him on a whim and be off to see the whole country if I packed a lunch.

"And this is the reason it meant so much to me at that specific moment in time: I had earned that money when Momma was around. Then, bang," he skipped his palms together, sending the top one shooting out in front of him like a rocket, "she wasn't. A page in the book of my life had turned, and I was a child no longer."

He craned his leathery neck and peered down at me. "At age ten, I needed something mine-all-mine. What could be better than a tool I could use for my emancipation?"

"Emancipation."

"You know, freedom."

"Yessir. I know."

"The Mud Cub spoke to me without words under those electric lights, boy, whispering about adventures we would have together, about rides on roads where it would be me and him and dirt ribbons wending through forests. About how he would get me a job being the paperboy around here, maybe make me rich, too.

"Some of it was siren song stuff. Some of it wasn't." He pointed to my fish. "Pretty good. Run your hand along it to check if you left any scales. Good. Do the other side now."

I felt it and flipped it and began again, exhaling.

"The shopkeeper came in through a doorway in the wall behind the counter. He looked like a lion tamer. His black hair was oiled and parted down the middle, as was the style then, and he wore a handlebar moustache as black as coal. The sleeves of his shirt were dirty where they had been cuffed and rolled back over his arms, and he wore a dark green apron covering most of his skinny frame, wrapping around his waist and almost overlapping at his back. He said, 'What can Sal do for you today, huh?' His voice was sunshine and song. His eyes twinkled.

"I spoke right up and said, 'I'm interested in purchasing that bicycle, Mr. Sal.' I pointed to the Mud Cub.

"He glanced at it. Turning back toward me and my father, he became quiet for a moment. Then he said, 'This one? This one is not for sale.'"

Chapter 16

Jonathan

"If the Mud Cub wasn't for sale, how in the world did you ever manage to buy it?" I wondered aloud.

"Wait a while now, son," Granddad said. "It turns out Mr. Sal was being a clever salesman. This didn't stop me from feeling as if my stomach had been run through a threshing machine anyhow. But my father had seen right through Sal's sales technique—he told me to go outside while he talked with the man in the shop.

"Now I have an idea, Jonathan, of what they talked about in there, but I can't be sure. I can't be sure my father bent his ear about my mother, about how we'd buried her yesterday, and to go easy on a boy who had worked for two years saving for a bicycle, and how maybe it was destiny…but I have an idea.

"What happened?" I asked, dumbfounded.

"I spent maybe ten minutes under the awning out on the front stoop of the shop, watching the rain come down. I tell you, Jonathan, I had given myself over to the dream of the Mud Cub completely. I imagined what it would be like to ride my own Mud Cub in the rain, my pockets light and cool and bare, if you get my meaning."

I didn't. Granddad saw the blankness on my face.

"Listen. The longer you save your pennies, the hotter they get, 'til one day they begin to burn a hole in your pocket."

I raised my eyebrows in concern.

"Not literally. I just mean you want to spend what you have. It's an itch. The undisciplined man is like a city with a broken down wall. But the disciplined man has learned to master himself. At least more often than not."

"Oh."

"Long story short, when my father called me back into the shop, Sal was changed. His moustache drooped lower at the corners. The Mud Cub had been pulled down from its display, and Sal quietly went about the business of fitting him to me as best he could. He lowered the seat as far as it would go and rotated the handlebars downward a bit, then told me to swing a leg over. And I did."

Granddad chucked the useful remains of a fish into the cooler. "It was total victory. I want to say that the shop disappeared around me, that my mind's eye saw a perfect summer day and a dry, smooth dirt road near home stretching out before the bars. I can still, even now, smell that moment in the old bicycle shop. The 3-in-1 oil, the rubber of the tires, the sawdust and packing crates. I still remember what he was like when he was new."

"Granddad?"

"Yes?"

"Why do you call the Mud Cub a 'he'?"

He chuckled. "Because for a long while, he was my best friend. And a boy isn't supposed to make friends like that with girls."

I didn't say anything.

"Not to say he doesn't anyhow." He gave me a sly look, one I would get used to, one I would learn to love and miss when he was gone. "At least not until it's appropriate." He gave a chuckle. "It was two years later, when I was twelve, that I knew Alice Benjamin was going to be my best friend for the rest of my life. That was when he—the ol' Mud Cub here —saw it was time to let go. Reluctantly. She had become everything to me."

Granddad's face became entirely earnest then, and he looked away, closed his eyes, and straightened up a little. "Truth is…she was my queen. Still is."

I got goosebumps because I knew he wasn't talking to me.

Chapter 17

Jonathan

I couldn't sleep that night, so I snuck out. The bedside clock showed a few minutes past one. I exited by the back door, barefoot in shaggy grass, making my way toward the Cadillac and the Mud Cub under the blackest blue eternity, stars scattered throughout.

These seeds of light were witnesses to my ache.

I was heartsick.

I missed my mother.

I missed my father, in a way, but the ache in my heart about him was separate, different.

For my mother I felt longing.

For my father I felt regret.

Toward my mother I flung nets to catch what comforts I could.

Toward my father I held up a shield but was ready to throw it down in a moment—if only I were safe with him.

I stopped; I cast my gaze at the heavens. I heard rumors: there was no such thing as safety in this world. Safety was a myth. And only men were supposed to know, not boys. Only men could handle this knowledge; boys couldn't.

But I had caught my glimpses. I had my theories.

And already.

I knew truths I wasn't supposed to know yet, and that knowledge had produced a wound. It was both obvious and ugly.

I walked down the hill and opened the heavy door to the shop. It took all my muscle to slide it enough to slip inside. I fumbled for the switch.

When the light came on, it was blinding. My eyes flexed, and I beheld that lovely gleaming cluster of torpedoes shaped in black, the naked chromium goddess at her fore, the bench and bicycle beyond.

I entered into the holy of holies.

I walked around the '39, looking and not touching, doing a full lap, feeling as if I were stealing things and loving the sensation. I sat at my stool, palms down on the seat between my legs, leaning forward and staring at her. I swear she stared right back. She *was*. And she was not ashamed to *be*.

This spell did not grow old, but just in case I could run it out, I decided to save some. So I turned away from her, toward the bicycle, toward the bench and shoebox with the old photographs inside.

There was one photograph of a girl in there, and she was so beautiful she seemed to come right off the paper.

Part 3: Granddad

Chapter 18

Malachi

I woke to find Jonathan gone. I admitted a brief stab of anxiety, but after punching its ticket, I gained control over it and began to search for facts.

I hadn't felt these kinds of feelings in years.

Jonathan's bibs were draped over the chair in his room. His boots were there in the mudroom right next to mine. I checked through the back window and saw that the door to the shop had been slid aside enough to perhaps admit the entrance of a twelve-year-old boy named Jonathan.

I grunted and went to brew the coffee.

The rooster began crowing not much later, and I thought the boy wouldn't be too long now. I poured myself the first cup.

He soon came boldfaced into the kitchen in his pajamas, barefoot with haystack hair, acting like he owned the place. That was the first time I thought about the will. "Couldn't sleep?"

"No, sir." He sat opposite from me at his end of the table and propped himself up on his elbows.

"Did you sleep at all?"

"I slept in the Cadillac, sir." He faced out the open windows toward the meadow and the shop and the creek and the trees beyond.

"Hm. Coffee?"

Razor-sharp blue eyes darted up to meet my own. "Really?"

"Why not, after all?" I stood and moved toward the percolator on the stove. "You could probably use it."

"I've never had coffee. Momma won't let me."

"What, says it'll stunt your growth?" I poured him a steaming mug and set it before him.

"Yes, sir."

I moved to sit back down. "Momma ain't here, is she?"

"Nope."

I let this one slide. I watched as he took a sip. I had to stifle my reaction to his first taste.

He asked—so I told him the rest of the story over our coffee—about Sal. I told him how the old bicycler had made it clear I was buying the very first Mud Cub and how special it was, how he couldn't imagine selling it to a better or more deserving person. He had charged me two whole dollars more than was listed on the price tag for that privilege, though—bringing the total to $14. Two years' wages, almost, traded in for a stab at…well, at immortality.

"How'd you get him all the way home to Tennessee?" he asked.

"Oh, I got the fool idea I could race and beat my father home from the station in Nashville."

"On the *bike*?"

"Yes."

"What happened?"

"It about killed me, but I rode the distance. I remember how my father squinted at me as he considered allowing me to attempt riding sixty miles on a bicycle. In the end I guessed he thought I needed to test myself. And his one condition was that we both stick to the same route. I thought it was out of a concern for fair play, but as I came of age it dawned on me that he had been trying to make sure he could watch over me."

"How long did it take?"

"Do you know how strong a breezy headwind can feel on a bicycle when you've been riding a whole day? What a difference it makes when the wind is with you as opposed to against you?"

The boy didn't answer. As I've said, he's bright.

"Sunup to sundown. My father made sure to send me with enough bread in my satchel to last me a while. And I stopped off at every creek and stream I could find to drink water."

"What was it like, Granddad?"

"The best and worst thing ever. I was a world master. At times, on some stretches where the sun was just right, I was the only one living in it. At other times my hindquarters were so raw I couldn't sit anymore."

A shamefaced grin passed across his face.

"In the end I learned there's little difference between hero and fool. The line is thin and can be crossed easily, even without intention. When I say it about killed me, I'm not using hyperbole. It really is possible to die of a bicycle ride."

The kid smiled, but it wasn't mirth; it was awe.

"Come on. We've got animals to feed. And bicycle maintenance needs to be done."

Chapter 19

Malachi

We found the stable a wreck.

I figured that a fox or maybe a raccoon or two had raided my henhouse.

There were feathers everywhere. Blood and the residue of animal fear flecked the place. The eggs were all gone. I counted only four hens.

My old philanderer strutted and crowed in warning tones in the corner.

Jonathan buzzed, up on the balls of his feet. I could feel in the air that this little episode hadn't yet concluded; the intruder might still be here.

"Jonathan," I said. "Standing in the corner by the fireplace in the living room is my twelve-gauge. Go and get it."

He turned, but before he could sprint off, I grabbed him by the strap of his bibs and stuck my face right into his. "Hey," I said, "it's loaded. Keep your finger off the trigger and the barrel pointed at the ground, understand?"

"Yes, sir," he said. And he was gone.

"Well how-dee, my old philandering cock," I said. "You *were* crowing differently this morning, come to think of it." I reached for the pitchfork and held the tines out low in front of me as I closed in on the henhouse. "Let's see if you managed to save any more, old fella."

I moved slow, pitchfork first, peering through the little door into the roosting area. There was a white puff in there, which could have been a whole dead hen or leftovers from the predator's dinner.

I spied out the rest of the inside, moving from one side to the other, my tines right at the door. I had almost satisfied myself that the four-legged raiding party had beat feet unscathed when I heard the growl.

I froze.

The rooster flapped his way toward me, agitated. "Get back, you old fool." I couldn't tell for sure if the growl had come from inside the coop or someplace else.

I was about to lift the henhouse lid when, in the distance, I heard the shotgun go off.

Chapter 20

Malachi

I left the stable gate flapping in the breeze, pitchfork discarded, and ran like a far younger man up the hill toward the house.

I busted in the back door wheezing and old, my heart racing with panic. The air in my house had turned stifling and smelled of cordite, pepper mixed with rotten egg.

I rounded the corner.

Jonathan was on his knees in the living room, hands clasped to his ears and crying.

"Jonathan, are you okay?" I was still trying to catch my breath in the acrid air as I knelt before him and took him by the shoulders. "Jonathan."

He gasped and opened his eyes. He was scared.

"Are you hurt?"

He pointed behind me.

I turned to look. There on the floor I saw my old twelve-gauge, its muzzle smoking and pointed toward us. My joints blazing, I walked to the gun, clicked the safety on, and stood it up in the corner.

"Jonathan," I panted, leaning against the wall for support, "I'm going to ask this only once more: are you hurt?" My lungs were on fire. I wanted to collapse.

"No, sir," he sobbed, his breaths coming quick and unsteady.

I gave us a moment. I double-checked the gun. It was safe. "What in *the hell* happened, boy?"

He stood and tried to compose himself, his hand reaching out limp as his index finger accused the gun. "I tripped," he sobbed. "I fell, and it went off when I—when I dropped it."

I looked around for evidence. "Where did the shot go? Oh." I saw it when I looked up. The plaster in a section of the ceiling was Swiss cheese overhead. "Hell*fire.*"

"Granddad please stop cussing!" he burst out, one word right on top of the other. Then he shrugged inward on himself, hiding his face behind one hand.

And that was pretty much the end of that moment.

Chapter 21

Malachi

The fox—or the coon or whatever—was gone. I was more bent out of shape about that than I was about the stupid hole in my living room ceiling.

I cracked open a root beer for the boy and gave it to him. I stuck to water. Especially after my run up the hill.

I opened a window. "House smells like a damn firing range. You sure you're not hurt?"

"Yes, sir."

"You're not bleeding anywhere?"

He said, "Only out of my ears," and rubbed them.

"You hear that high-pitched whine, the ringing?"

"Yes, sir."

"It'll go away."

A pause. "Sir?"

"Yes."

"I'm sorry. I didn't mean to—"

"I forgive you, Jonathan. It was an honest mistake." I looked at him. "Right?"

He looked at me. "Yes, sir."

"And no harm done."

"Except the ceiling."

"Well," I shrugged, "you can fix it later." I watched as this responsibility loaded itself and settled down onto his shoulders. I reckoned he would manage it okay.

"Granddad, what killed the chickens?"

"I'd be God darned if I know," I said, deep in thought, squeezing the water from my teeth as I drew my lips tight against them, making a sucking sound. "I was about to find out when all of a sudden my house exploded."

He nodded, took a sip of root beer from his bottle, let his eyes wander outside the windows, and said, "Damn."

I shook my head and smiled, exhaling a short blast through my nostrils. "Yeah, you might say so. But we'll find 'im, boy. We'll find him, and we'll kill 'im. Took two of our hens; I have every right. Maybe we'll set a trap for him. Then we see what we get."

"What do you think it was, sir?"

"Fox, maybe. Raccoon, probably. We need to go check it out, see what kind of facts we can dig up. You up for solving a mystery?"

"Yes, sir."

"Good. Bring the shotgun." This time I showed him how to carry it, and I made good and sure the safety was on. I also made him walk in front of me. Little city boy.

Chapter 22

Malachi

"Look there," I said, pointing at a space under the chicken wire. "Something dug its way in."

"What's that mean?"

"It rules out the coon idea. They would climb up and in. And—wait a while—now I'm not so sure about the fox." I thought about it.

"Granddad, that looks like what a dog would do. Our dog likes to dig under the fence. I've had to go find her a lot."

"A dog, huh? Well. That is interesting." The kid was sharp. "Some kind of canine, huh? Maybe it was a fox after all."

I decided to set a trap every night and see about it. Meanwhile, we fixed up the coop and the henhouse. We searched the property and eventually found our two dead hens. That too was significant; it was a clue: a fox would take its kill, not leave it to rot.

But I said nothing. We stuck the carcasses in a barrel and burned them along with some bits of brush.

While we were at it and I was thinking about making burn piles, I officially added the outhouse project to Jonathan's list of chores. "Tear it down, stack it in the middle of the meadow, and we'll burn it after a good rain. Use the cart over by the shop to move it. I'll show you."

There were no eggs that day. And I was sure there probably wouldn't be any for a few days more, 'til the hens settled down and I could keep them from being terrorized.

After the animals were released to engage what was left of their routine, I took Jonathan to the shop.

I had to dig for a while to find my bicycle repair stand. Jonathan helped me shuffle it from the corner over to the bench.

"First things first," I said. "He's been sitting idle for decades, so we need to get some penetrating oil on his nuts and bolts, loosen him up some."

I handed the boy the can of lubricant and showed him how to get a spritz on every exposed bit of machine thread he could find on the bike, starting with the seatpost binder. "We need that one to work first so we can raise the seat enough to get him the stand, get the bicycle off the ground, see."

"You sure know a lot about everything," Jonathan said.

I had to chuckle at that. "I got a good lead on ya; it's alright. You're sharp."

"Well, thanks for teaching me, Granddad. I appreciate it."

"You're a good boy, Jonathan."

Pretty soon Mud Cub One was hanging by his seatpost in the stand, ready for attention.

Chapter 23

Malachi

We "broke" the chain and coiled it up at the bottom of a coffee can to soak it in 90-weight, oil so thick it flowed down from the can looking like a golden ribbon of cold honey, immersing the chain in its sweetness. I set this little industrial stew over on the hot plate and said, "The heat will go to work, letting the oil get in there and clean things up."

"How long do we leave it like that?"

"All day. I'll turn it off at night, but it may need another session tomorrow." I tipped the can toward me and peered in. "And maybe an oil change."

We stripped the tires from the rims and shot the spoke nipples with penetrating oil so I could start truing them. I set the kid to work with a spray bottle of water and some rags, cleaning the frame and fork.

I gave the front axle a spin. "Hear that? Sounds like there's rocks in there?"

"Yes, sir."

"It's dry as a bone. We're gonna have to rebuild it. Grab me that tin of grease there." I pointed.

Jonathan placed the grease on the benchtop. "What now?"

"Sit here," I said, "and grab that wheel." He did. "Now with this wrench on this nut and the other on the cone, work 'em opposite from one another until they let go." I showed him.

"What's the cone?"

"The inner race."

"What's that?"

"Where the ball bearings run and support the weight of the hub. You'll see when we get him apart."

Our work went on like this.

"I suppose it's time I teach you how to fire a gun." I looked over the tops of my glasses at him as we worked. "Ever shot one before?"

"Just today."

"That don't count. Doesn't count, excuse me. When we get to a stopping point in here today, we'll set up some targets for you."

The boy turned toward me, a question on his face that didn't quite get to his lips. I liked that about the kid, that he was slow to speak, but I sensed that he thought it was a flaw and didn't appreciate it the way he ought to. "What is it?"

"Do you have those earmuff things?"

"Well now, wait a while." I continued working. It took most of five minutes before it finally came to me. "Yeah, I suppose they're over by the grinding wheel, come to think of it."

"I wanna use 'em. That shotgun is damned loud."

"Watch your language, Jonathan. Profanity doesn't suit children."

"Can I say damn when I'm a man?"

"Didn't you just? Anyhow, it's not something you need right now. Words like that become appropriate under pressure."

He was quiet. Then, "Haven't I been through some stuff?"

"Well, now…I suppose you have." I grunted. "I'm not ready to hear it coming from your virgin lips, however. I'm trying to help grow you up into a *good* man, Jonathan."

"How come it's not wrong for you?"

"I've killed before. And I ain't no virgin." That shut him up. "Some things you've got to earn. At least around the Forty."

I then changed the subject. "We'll head up into the city tomorrow and get the parts we need. We'll have to go all the way up to Nash. Nobody around Columbia is going to have parts that fit him. You can wear your city clothes, and we'll put up in a mo-tel and come back the next day."

"Granddad?"

"Yes, son?"

"Is it okay if I wear my bibs? I like them."

"No. A respectable man dresses up at least a little when he goes to the city. You'll see."

After supper I spaced out a few milk jugs filled with water on some old bales against the woods over by the shop. I walked off thirty yards and made a line in the grass with my boot.

"You ought to be able to hit a gnat's eyelash at this range with the Winchester," I told the boy. "But the shotgun's got a spread and is better closer. Its effects are also more obvious."

I racked all six shells out of the magazine and helped Jonathan get good and cozy with the empty twelve-gauge.

"You want the butt stock firmly wedged into your shoulder here," I said. "And always keep your finger straight and off the trigger until you're ready to fire. And never aim at anything you do not intend to shoot."

I made him repeat those things several times until I was sure he understood them. "A gunshot wound ain't nothing special, but it will kill. Most of what's scary is the bang," I lied.

There are times a man lies and can't justify it beyond trying to protect those he loves. I figured the righteous did their best and left the sorting to God.

Jonathan took the weapon. I made him dry-fire it several times to get him used to the feel of the trigger and where it let go in its travel.

"Control your breathing, son. In, out, in, out, and hold. Then squeeze —don't pull—the trigger. Slow, steady squeeze."

The trigger clicked.

"That's right. Right there, the shell will fire. If you relax and let the weapon work with your body, you'll hit what you aim at every single time. Keep it tight to your shoulder or you'll have your arm in a sling for days."

I showed him how to load it and how to rack the slide.

Then we went live.

I handed him the earmuffs. At thirty yards with birdshot, Jonathan exploded six of seven milk jugs.

"Beginner's luck," I told him, but the kid was a natural. I wasn't about to tell him that yet. Kid had it in his Green blood.

Chapter 24

Malachi

The next morning, there were no eggs.

We ate a different breakfast.

I dressed in slacks and wore my city shoes. I donned my straw fedora (the one with the little orange feather) as well as my cardigan, and we walked out the door.

The boy wore blue jeans and a t-shirt. His generation didn't have a clue about propriety.

These things could be trained in, though. At least I hoped.

The first thing we did when we drew near to Nashville was book our room—a double on the first floor of a Travelodge right off Route 31.

I telephoned a few bicycle shops from the yellow section of the book and wrote down addresses. I bought a map of metropolitan Nashville from the rack by the front desk, then we took a late lunch at the old diner up the way. After that, we headed into the city.

I floored the Chevy merging onto the freeway, which provoked a look from Jonathan. As if I were doing something wrong. "You've gotta blow the carbon out every once in a while." That was what I told him.

He didn't say anything, but that was alright. It was perfectly fine for a man to enjoy a little wide open throttle now and then.

When we walked into at the bicycle shop, which was a little hole-in-the-wall operation, I glanced around. It looked like a one-man show, which took me back to Sal's shop all over again. It was funny how life came at you in waves, and how one wave could be so much like another that it moved you from the moment you were in to one you hadn't thought of for decades. Especially when the smells were the same. Rubber and oil and steel.

Then a door behind the counter opened, and a young woman in cutoff jean shorts and a skintight t-shirt emerged. "Can I help you?" she asked. Visions of Sal's shop fizzled to ignominy, along with my smile.

I assumed the woman worked there. It was either that or she had taken a break from turning tricks in the street.

I introduced myself and held out my hand.

She shook it limply, as if obligated but annoyed by the formality. She didn't give me her name; I had to ask it: Betsy.

She had neither the decency nor the good sense, however obvious to some of us, to wear a bra under her shirt.

I couldn't help but notice, and it outraged me. But some people were instigators and made it their business to do all they could to tempt, to derail anyone and everyone around them. *This world is going straight to hell.*

It mostly pissed me off, I realized, because Jonathan was with me. This stupid girl, this Betsy, was going to force me into conversations I wasn't ready to have with him yet. What gave her the right to make ordinary life so costly for the people around her?

I wanted to get right in her face and ask her how she could dare such a thing, whether her conscience was seared.

If the boy had to learn about prostitutes or pornography, it should have been up to me to decide the timing, or even for him to ask, but not for her to use this kind of force. *Dammit!* I hated people who stole, especially from me and my family. And she was stealing innocence—one of the most precious things under the sun—however little he had left.

But was there actually one innocent man under the sun? No. What we called innocence was closer to ignorance, and it really was bliss. And once it was gone, you could never get it back.

It took some effort to avert my eyes as I gave Betsy my personal card —which communicated both my name and mailing address—and told her that I'd telephoned earlier about the parts for the Mud Cub.

She pocketed my card and led us to the parts counter.

On it a sack of items, plus two tires, awaited us.

A bicycle mechanic was truing a wheel at the bench, but he didn't look at us. He was watching Betsy as she bounced toward the register. Casual lust crawled over him like he was filing away a slideshow for later, when he'd be alone.

What scum.

But I'd made a discipline of ignoring foolish boys. "I'm glad you had these parts in stock," I said to Betsy, making an attempt at small talk. I was trying to endure the crucible so we could make it out the door before something regrettable happened. "You can't find these odd sizes anywhere anymore."

But maybe something regrettable had happened already. I felt like Jonathan and I had been ambushed.

"Yeah, dude," she said. "That English stuff is pretty rare." She leaned forward and set her elbows on the counter, enhancing the view.

I didn't know if this enhancement was intentional or not, but it exasperated me, and I sighed roughly. She was forcing me to cross the Rubicon.

"Listen, Betsy. Here's the deal. I suppose I could blame your parents for failing to teach you manners or to respect your elders. But I suppose I could blame you, since you have zero respect for yourself." I couldn't stop a gesture that was aimed generally at her indiscretion.

"Either way—whether you weren't taught polite behavior or you've rejected it for your own reasons—you have to know that the indiscretions you commit don't just cost you. They cost everyone around you."

She stared at me, mostly with stupidity at first, but as the light dawned on her countenance, stupidity acquiesced, stepped aside, and revealed hatred—which had been present from the word go. "Hey. Just what are you saying, old guy?"

I shook my head. "I hate to belabor the obvious," I pointed now, "but I think you forgot to put on some of your clothes this morning. Come on, miss. We don't need to see that."

She glanced down and back up. The light, now fully energized, was nevertheless dim. She stepped behind the register and began ringing me up. "Whatever. Let's get you out of here."

I paused and breathed. *Is it worth the argument?* I wondered. Alice would have said it was, but she would also have been gracious, if firm.

She would have been eloquent.

And she would have made a difference. *How I wish she were still here.*

I rested my palms on the edge of the counter. "Betsy—it is Betsy, isn't it?"

"Yeah," she said, cocking a hip at me and glancing at the register. "Your total is $42.78. Will it be check, cash, or charge?"

I wanted to tell her that a member of the fairer sex as selfish as she was took all the pleasure out of being anywhere near her, but I bridled my yap. "Cash." I handed her a fifty, unable to avoid glancing at her chest, unable to avoid saying, "If you were my daughter, young lady, I'd —"

"You'd what?" She was belligerent now.

I lowered my voice and turned my face aside. "Why…I'd be ashamed of you."

Silence.

There was shuffling and clinking as she made my change. She didn't count it out to me, and I felt like counting it, so I took the time to do it.

"Okay. Listen, Betsy," I said, grabbing the tires and handing them off to the kid. "I'll say one more thing, then we'll go and never come back.

"This ain't your world, honey. It won't be until all the men like me finally die off, and when we do, it'll finally catch fire. Because of people like you. Until then, can you show yourself enough respect to dress appropriately? If not for you or even for me, then at least for the kid?"

She pointed over my shoulder. "There's the door." The words came through gnashed teeth.

"Keep your shirt on." I turned to the boy. "Come on, Jonathan. Let's go." I sighed as I held the door open. "Anyhow, I want to buy you a butter pecan sugar cone."

Then Jonathan and I walked out. And never looked back.

Coming back into the light took some time, forgetting, and letting go. Because I hated injustice with every fiber of my being, I'd always had trouble with that last one.

But butter pecan ice cream helped. It usually did.

Chapter 25

Malachi

It was several days before much more of note happened. Life went on as it does.

It took me some time to think on what, specifically, I wanted to say to Jonathan about women. I'd had a daughter; Sarah and I had talked about boys and men. And I knew quite a bit about both, but I'd never had to have The Talk with a boy about girls.

Since Jonathan's dirtbag father wasn't around, it fell to me now, and I felt like delaying.

I'd been setting traps nightly by the henhouse. It was a whole lot of nothing for the first couple of nights, but one morning we discovered nibbles in our bait. This wasn't enough activity to set off the trap, but one of the marshmallows had been taken (crafty bastards), and there was a whole lot of disturbance in the grass where I had dumped the oil from one of my sardine tins.

I decided to leave a whole can of them open right there inside the trap that night.

The Mud Cub was taking shape. He wasn't much to look at as far as I was concerned, but I could tell Jonathan was stricken by him good and hard. Jonathan didn't have the filter of my memories; he didn't know how magnificent the bike had been on that showroom floor. To him, it was magnificent now.

And he was becoming acquainted with beauty.

I sat at the truing stand, straightening out the rear wheel. "What did you think about that young woman at the shop the other day? She was pretty, huh?"

"Nah," he said. "She didn't catch my eye."

I stopped what I was doing and faced him square. "How could she not catch your eye, son?"

"I don't like women like that."

I thought about the will again. "Alright. Tell me what you mean."

He blushed. "Do I have to say it, Granddad?"

"Sure," I winked. "How else am I gonna know what you're talking about?"

He held his hands out in a gesture that meant the point he was trying to make was too obvious. "She wasn't even wearing a bra. What kind of lady is that?"

I smirked. "You noticed that, uh."

"How could I not notice it?"

"Yes indeed." I decided to redirect the subject.

"I may have sounded like I was playing the tyrant in that bike shop, boy, but I wasn't. They don't know how cruel they are toward us sometimes.

"Cruel?"

"Absolutely, yes. Women are powerful creatures, son. They sure are, in their own way. Some of them have grasped that and chosen to misuse it, too. Those women become repellent, at least to a good man. They aren't powerful; they're dangerous. In every kind of way."

"What are you *actually* saying, Granddad?"

"Well, now, wait a while." I paused. *That's one helluva question.*

"There's an old saying," I said, "that goes, 'If you wanna double your money, best thing to do is fold it over and stick it back in your pocket.'" I glanced up at him over the tops of my glasses.

He was blank.

"Sometimes it's best to hang on to what you've got, in other words. Even if it's stark raving ignorance."

"I don't get it."

"I'm saying you want to avoid the type of woman who throws herself at you. Or worse, who wants to punish you for being a man. A good woman is a treasure worthy of the chase. That broad at the bicycle shop didn't have enough self-respect to lift herself—or what she has been given—above cheap sex. That's on the bottom shelf."

He had glued himself to his work, busting rust on the chrome handlebar with a wad of steel wool. "I don't know what you mean."

"That's good, son. That's a good thing. Listen, Jonathan. Look at me."

He did.

"There are things in this world you can't unlearn. There are things you'll see that you can't unsee, though one day you'll wish with all your heart you could. The best cure for that kind of injustice is time.

"You'll walk rough paths; every man does. What matters is how you handle yourself on 'em. Remember that old saw about doubling your money."

I paused to think, then continued. "One of the measures of a man is how he behaves under pressure. There are many kinds of pressure, and each man has his—well, his kryptonite."

"Superman." The boy was getting it.

"Right. The comic came way before the movie, so you know."

"I do."

I believed him. "Some men manifest a certain weakness under the pressure of conflict. It's not the weakness which is common to every man; I'm talking about something darker. They run, they buckle; they're cowards and rebels and traitors at their core. Like that mechanic fella working on the wheel at the bike shop. Did you notice his eyes?"

"Yes, sir. He let 'em go all over her body."

"Exactly. He was taking something from her that wasn't his to have. Even if it seemed she was giving it out to anyone who'd have it. In fact, she had trapped him with that power I'm talking about. Worse, she was either too stupid or too broken to feel any shame about it. Zero self-respect.

"She'd probably say she's exercising her freedom. I've heard it all before. But she's just as much a slave as her admirers. All kinds of things can go on in a man's mind about a girl who—well, let's face it—might as well have been half-naked, right?"

Jonathan blushed.

"You've got to try to control those thoughts, son. Sometimes work can be your best friend when those kinds of thoughts are running wild in you." I pointed toward his groin. "That's going to start voicing its opinion about certain matters soon." I paused. "If it hasn't already. You don't make decisions with that. A man thinks with his head and feels with his heart. The rest is reserved for his bride and only his bride."

I thought some more.

"Jonathan, I know I'm saying a lot right now. I want you to know that… a good woman is a flawed goddess who needs…she's in need of a champion, boy. She's virtuous. Beautiful. And worthy of the good man who wills himself to commit to her. She walks in emanations of mystery, leaving to the imaginations of lesser, unworthy men what she reserves in truth for her noble lover.

"And love, like authority—like faith—is a thing never taken, never forced. These things can only be freely given, freely received. She's as fragile and tender as an open bloom, in need of a good man to shelter her beauty with his love. If she's worthy, she knows she's in need of his strength, and that she doesn't resist her innate delicacy makes her all the more lovely.

"Listen, Jonathan: the secret of manhood is that men were made to serve."

"Why, Granddad?"

"Because we're strong. And strength has a need to serve. Which is why it's so easily abused."

He stopped to consider that awhile. "What are women made for?"

"Woman were made to help man use his strength well. It's not good for him to be alone. She is the place where his strength can find rest and life. See how they need one another to be whole?"

"Yes, sir. Is that how it was for you and Grandma Alice?"

I was unprepared to hear her name. It stunned me. My throat became dry, my voice quiet. "Yeah, boy." I swallowed. "Yeah. That's how it was." What I couldn't say was that, because she had been gone so long, I'd almost forgotten some of my most important lessons.

The truth was, I was as good as dead before this little disrupter had come to the Forty. Like a messenger of God. Reminding me how small I was.

Part 4: Jonathan

Chapter 26

Jonathan

Granddad woke me by shouting my name up the stairs at 5:30 a.m. I thought I was having a heart attack. I flew out of bed, tripping on the quilt, and ran to the top of the stairs. "What is it?"

"Get dressed. We got 'im."

"Who?"

"The coon. Quick. Hurry."

I ran back for my bibs and jumped into them without a shirt. The rivets were cold against the skin of my chest.

I raced down the stairs.

The door had slammed shut on me, but I plowed through it to behold Granddad walking away at speed in the distance, his shotgun in his right hand. I crammed his old floppy hat on my head and shucked into my boots sockless.

I was Tom Sawyer.

I sprinted to catch up.

When we got to the henhouse, the trap was on its side and twitching about. The animals were in an uproar. The rooster crowed ominously, the hens cackled and flapped. The stalls in the stable trembled.

I also heard the short rasp of a dog barking. The animal in the cage was as white as chalk—a ghost.

"What is that thing?"

"Aw, not again."

"What?"

"We caught the Munro dog." He said it like he said mo-tel, with all the emphasis on the first syllable.

I was breathless and confused. "How did we do that?"

Granddad half-raised the gun and said softly, "To kill or not to kill?" He finally hung his head. "Dadgummit. I can't shoot that stupid thing."

"Let it out first, then."

"No, Jonathan. I mean there'd be hell to pay with the Munroes. That's Shyla, their little pet terrier." He turned toward the dog. "Aren't you, you little bloodthirsty egg-sucking bitch?" He kicked the trap.

The dog whined and tucked her tail.

Granddad stood and appeared to mull his options, leaning the gun up against the fence. He rubbed his face with both hands as he thought.

After a few moments, he seemed to have made a decision. "Alright. We'll take the Cadillac. We'll go right now. Pick up that twelve-gauge, boy. I'll get the stupid dog."

We walked our cargo toward the shop.

"Hang on. I've got to get some cardboard down in the trunk, or she may piss all over everything and raise a stink."

"Why don't we take the Chevy?" I leaned the shotgun up against the tool bench, our base of operations.

"Because I've decided we're going to make an impression. And if this car does one thing, it certainly does that." He turned to the dog. "Damn you, Shyla, why do you want to make so much work for me? You little rat, you stole all my eggs and killed two of my hens. Now your master's gonna have to reckon with your sins." He slammed the trunk lid home over the little cage. The dog yipped and fell silent.

I'd never seen Granddad this way; I was both afraid of him and mesmerized.

And if I'd always wanted to go for a ride in the Cadillac, under these circumstances I was torn. It must have been destiny because against my own howling will, I ended up in the car with him.

I would have many more out-of-body experiences in regard to my will as I grew to be a man.

But today—in which I was a mere twelve years old—would only get worse as it went.

The car was alive, tingling with power from the first crank of the starter. Granddad became yet another man I didn't know as he backed it out of the shop and guided it down the drive toward County Line Road.

The naked chromium goddess showed us the way.

It was a short drive made long because it was done in silence. Except for the dog in the trunk.

With every yip and whine, Granddad's scowl deepened. It might have been fifteen minutes, but it felt like an hour.

(There were no seat belts.)

We came to the right place and cruised up the tree-lined gravel drive of the Munro property toward their house.

It was a two-story fortress of rusty brick and bone-white columns. A big bronze plaque with an M on it was bolted to the wall by the front doors. It'd be a few years before I'd figured out the usual *accouterments* of ambition and pretense, but these were them for sure.

Granddad parked right out front—as if he owned the place and the Munroes were his tenants.

He was gentle opening the trunk lid but not in extracting the cage from its environs. He flung the pee-stained sheet of cardboard into the shrubs. "Come on, Jon."

I accompanied him to the doors, where he rang the bell. At length, a short, balding man answered. He was in a bathrobe. Gray curlicues sprouted from the V it made at his chest, and his magnified eyes hid behind large glasses. "Why, Malachi. It's you. It's early."

"Yes, Frank. It's me. This is your little bitch, isn't it?" He held the caged dog up like a fish on a stringer, and it whined. "Unless, of course, you won't lay claim to her for the grief she's caused me."

"What did you do to her? Why is she in a coon trap?"

"Now wait a minute. I lost two hens to this mangy, no-good rat. Plus all my eggs. My hens still won't lay, all the ruckus she's caused over at the Forty."

Frank raised his eyebrows. "Oh." He saw the Cadillac back behind and between us, framed by the shrubs and our figures. His overlarge eyes darted back to Granddad.

"I tell you what, Frank. This is a courtesy call. I damn near shot her right inside my trap, but I didn't want there to be animosity between us. You know also that I could have killed her and never told you, but I'm a man of honor."

Granddad tripped the trap's lever and dumped the dog out at the threshold. "And what's yours is yours to deal with."

She scrambled on the oak floor, her claws tick-tacking as she fled deep into the house. "Do I need to tell you what's going to happen if I find her on my property one more time?"

"No, sir," Frank Munro said with solemnity, and I could tell he meant every syllable.

For the first time that day, my granddad smiled. "Good. And good day to you, Mr. Munro." First syllable again. He turned, and I followed.

The Cadillac was still running, the trunk lid still up. As we walked back toward the car, Granddad sniffed the trap and made a face. "Smells like dog piss." He stopped. For a second, I thought he was going to pitch it in with the cardboard when Mr. Munro called out.

"Mr. Green, hold on a minute. I just remembered…that boy there. Is his name Jonathan?"

Granddad froze. Then he turned back around and faced Frank.

They were fifty feet apart at each end of the walkway, Frank still in his doorway at the top of the front porch. "How'd you know his name?"

This was the O.K. Corral; Granddad was Wyatt, and I was Doc. Frank Munro was Billy Clanton. And somebody was about to die.

"Fella came around asking the other day. Said he was lost, that he was trying to find his way to a surprise visit with his family. Said he had a blue-eyed boy named Jonathan, about his age, maybe twelve." He pointed at me.

That finger might as well have belonged to the angel of death.

Granddad towered over me. That was the first time I ever saw fear on his face. And pain. There was pain, too.

The coon trap did end up in the shrubs with the cardboard.

"Get in," he said, "let's go."

Chapter 27

Jonathan

The Cadillac wafted us through the Tennessee countryside, and I sat up front beside my grandfather with the vent window open, trying to breathe.

"You told him where you'd be?"

"Yes, sir."

"Jon, the whole point of you coming here to the Forty was so that he couldn't find you, boy. Why did you tell him?"

"He asked." I began to choke on my emotions. "Mom wasn't home. She was at work. He hadn't called in forever, and when he finally did, he was so nice. He asked me what was new in my life and if he could visit me, but I told him I was going away, and he asked where to, and then—" I broke down and sobbed, my face in my lap.

I felt Granddad's hand come around and rough up the hair on the back of my head, then he patted me on the shoulder.

A long moment passed, then he cursed low and breathed deep.

"Hey, Jon."

He paused again.

"Guess what," he said. "1 lied."

I turned to him in a panic. "What? You lied? What do you mean?"

"About the whole point of you coming here. It wasn't so he couldn't find you."

I waited with my brows crinkled. No words came to me, so I waited.

Then he spoke. "It was so you and I could find you."

Chapter 28

Jonathan

The rest of the day stung. Granddad's words echoed through me, a potent infusion of medicine. I tapped into it, and it slowly worked its way into the durable parts of me.

And I heard echoes of these things the next morning as I fed the hens.

I found an egg that morning, the first egg since Shyla. There was hope in that egg. I left it for the hen. I didn't know how long it took to make a new chicken, but I did know they had to keep their eggs warm until they hatched. So I left it for her.

When I told Granddad later about what I'd done, his eyes welled up, and he said what he sometimes said to me: "Jonathan, you're a good boy."

Except now he didn't call me by my young name.

He called me Jon. I liked that.

I decided I would start calling myself Jon. It sounded more grown-up, less like I was a momma's boy.

Jon I liked. I also liked it when Granddad called me son.

He was, I now knew, the dad I'd never had. He wasn't the dad I'd always wanted—he scared me a little. But it was good for me to be near him.

The next day the sting had ebbed a little, and I remembered how Granddad had said time was the only cure man had found for pain. He was right about that, as far as I could tell, but I also think the Mud Cub helped…because that was the first day I rode him.

Granddad released the bike stand's clamp, and the Mud Cub touched down ready to ride for the first time in three times as long as I'd been alive.

He lowered the seat all the way (the same as Sal had done for him), and the shop was flooded with beams from a humid sun, cutting through the slats and striping the Cadillac again.

"

Granddad was a lion tamer, the Mud Cub was a jungle cat, and I was Mowgli—and I would prowl around on County Line Road and find a hill and ride it, the rush and thrill bubbling through my blood and making it red, fire engine red.

Mud Cub red.

I became a true boy that day, the day I found freedom on two wheels. I didn't come home until after the sun's last rays had faded into obsidian and the waxing moon had risen in the east, its half-masque a testimony of the tension and pressure in the world.

I was awakening.

I was finding my strength. I knew I could be just as terrible as I chose; I could feel power rising within me. And it was awesome. I began to feel like a god, like a real man.

Chapter 29

Jonathan

It rained the next day.

After breakfast and chores (we left the henhouse gate open, but the hens stayed inside where it was dry), we scurried back up to the house where we too could be warm and dry.

Once we'd cleaned up a little, Granddad sat down in his recliner. He wore his slippers, an old pair of jeans, and a white t-shirt under a simple cardigan, and all he seemed to want in the whole wide world was to sit and read his book.

I crept upstairs and slipped into my jeans and a white t-shirt, too. I took some books from my bag, including *The Jungle Book,* and went back downstairs.

I took up my position in Grandma Alice's easy chair, which stood in its place like a monument next to Granddad's chair. I got the feeling I was being allowed to sit in it because Granddad actively allowed me to do so, which meant permission could be revoked at any instant.

Granddad glanced at me over the tops of his reading glasses and went back to reading for a moment. Then he stood and left the room.

He came back with a button-up cardigan for me. It was about the same color as his: split-pea green. "Put this on, son. It's cold today." Then he sat back down.

I put the sweater on like a uniform, and we read books in those chairs for most of the rest of the day.

When Granddad started snoring, I went to the kitchen and watched the rain come down a while, but then I returned to my room.

Mom had packed me a few toys. I hadn't played with them much since I'd arrived at the Forty. There was no time for it.

Now, as I set up my cars and trucks on the floor in my room, I felt sad. It was hard to deny the emptiness when it stared me down: I had forgotten how to play. Didn't I have the heart for it anymore?

In any case, it was difficult to concentrate on my cars with a bunch of shotgun-blasted holes in the floor.

I decided to change back into my bibs, grab a slicker, and take a ride in the rain. After a few runs down the long ruts in the driveway, I started to think about how cool it would be if there were snow here and I had a toboggan.

And then I began to dwell in a simmer of thoughts about how nice it would be if I were a grown man, the Forty was mine, and I could go down this hill with my kids in the winters.

That made me happy in a way I hadn't felt before.

Chapter 30

Jonathan

After chores the next day, the sun rose clear and bright. The fields awoke slow and dozy, hemmed by thick blankets of fog.

Granddad showed me the cart and the tools, then I got to work demolishing the old outhouse. He headed for the shop, leaving me alone, and I worked hard.

Before lunchtime, I'd finished piling up the wood in the meadow as he'd instructed. He splashed some diesel on the pile and allowed me to set it on fire with his Zippo. It burned quickly.

Soon there was nothing but ash.

Later we sat at the kitchen table over sandwiches and milk.

"Granddad, tell me about how you met Grandma Alice."

He put his sandwich down after a moment, squinted, and sucked air through his teeth with his tongue the way he did sometimes. His glass of milk remained untouched on the table (he wouldn't drink a drop during his meals; it was always for after). "What do you want to know?"

I had to think. "How it felt," I said.

He harrumphed. "I can't explain that. Not with words."

I felt the gate closing on me.

Granddad only talked about the stuff he wanted to talk about, and only when he was ready to talk about it. I feared irritating him, but I was desperate. About all this stuff I didn't know, about her, about the war, about how he became a man.

"Well, what did she look like? How did you meet?"

He sighed and took another bite of his sandwich.

I thought he was ignoring me, so I shifted my focus back to my own sandwich and began contemplating giving up on this conversation.

But then he spoke. "I was almost eleven. It was summer. June. In less than a year, I would realize that she was my best friend in the whole world. I'd been out to the Benjamin place a few times by now, and it wouldn't be long before I met her and everything changed."

"How did you meet?"

"We'll get there, son. Let me tell my story. Work had taken me farther away from home than ever. I had transportation, and word of mouth was growing my little business fast. Nineteen twenty-three, at least around here, wasn't that different from all the years that had gone before.

"People still needed the same things done, and generally speaking there weren't enough hours in the day during the working season to get them done. When they heard I did good work, they would either telephone the house, stop me on the road to hire me, or talk to a neighbor who had passed the word.

"Mr. Benjamin happened to be in need of help in the summer of twenty-three because he was planning on breeding hogs. He was building a new stable.

"He needed a helper, and I needed to learn a trade. Framing and finish carpentry were the kinds of things I had a knack for. It was a good match.

"That's not to say I was excited about learning framing for the sake of framing. It was work, and work is a different kind of enjoyable than what you might do for fun. It's not like playing."

"I think know what you mean," I said, remembering how I had found myself unable to play with my cars. Granddad's brows vee'd together like the windshield of the Cadillac.

"So I showed up for work not because I loved it but because it was the right thing to do. And because I'd given Mr. Benjamin my word. Every day, I would arrive at the Benjamin place—about ten miles from here—right after sunrise and find he'd been working already. We'd work from then until about one, at which point we would go to the house for lunch.

"One day, as we walked toward the house at lunchtime, we found a gathering of buggies and automobiles in the drive that hadn't been there before. I reckoned this new development meant they had company. When I asked him about it, he said it was another tea party his wife was putting on for some of the local ladies and their daughters.

"Now. Up to this point, I had not met Alice. I told Mr. Benjamin I'd rather take my lunch at the job site than go inside and suffer through all that clucking and gossip."

"What did he say then?"

"He told me to stuff it. And to remove my boots at the back stoop."

I could relate. "So, what happened then? Was Alice at the tea party?"

"No, she was not. But wait a while; you're getting ahead of me.

"Jon, I was spoiled for choice. There were cakes and puddings and desserts, things I couldn't have imagined even existed. My mother hadn't been a woman of fashion; she was never interested in European dress or fancy food.

"But Mrs. Benjamin was what you might call keen on those things. She appreciated and studied them, making it her hobby to decode what the aristocrats were eating and drinking and wearing in Paris. She was no snob; it was a simple fascination.

"There wasn't a soul for miles around who could match Mrs. Benjamin for her tea parties. And because of the food, once I was inside, I didn't want to go back out to work on the stable.

"As I prevaricated indoors, and since Mr. Benjamin had taken a walk to the outhouse—unusual because the worst time of day to visit the outhouse is in the afternoon, when the flies are thickest—I made my way toward the parlor door for some light eavesdropping.

"I was no momma's boy. I wasn't curious about women and how they were built and what made them tick. At most I was irritated at how oddly they acted and how they could be concerned with matters so trifling as what so-and-so thought about such-and-such. Hooey. But everything was about to change for me, boy.

"When I approached the wide-open parlor door, I paused well clear of entering the room. I stood three feet from the entrance with a glass of sweet tea in my hand and just listened to all the goings-on. I tell you, Jon, it was like trying to decipher a code I had no hope of breaking. It all went right over my head.

"Until, that is, I heard a gasp from a cluster of girls. They were about my age and huddled across the room with their backs to me. They were looking at a photograph I couldn't see clearly from where I stood.

"I heard someone exclaim, 'She's so beautiful!' Suddenly they were speaking my language, my ears were opened, I was interested, and my heart became hungry.

"I moved forward and peered past the jamb into the room, trying to catch a glimpse of what kind of woman would be so ravishing a creature as to cause a stir in her own kind. She had to be something special indeed.

"I came close enough to see. There were about five girls in a semicircle, one of them holding the photograph. The portrait showed a girl looking into the camera. She was the most beautiful expression of the feminine I had ever beheld.

"From that moment, I was gone. I couldn't help myself from asking aloud what her name was. They turned to look at me, a masculine intruder, with shock. 'Why, that's Alice Benjamin,' one of them said, and they burst out laughing as if I'd asked the stupidest question ever heard. Granddad smiled. "And in a way, I had."

"Why?" I asked.

"Because it could only ever have been her."

Chapter 31

Jonathan

I asked Granddad if that was when he had met her—at the tea party.

"She wasn't home," Granddad said. "She was away at the time and had been away, I would learn later, for six weeks. She was thirteen. She was traveling the western part of the country with her Aunt Tilda, who was like Alice's mother: cosmopolitan. Those feminine arts about which I understood so little. All I knew was that I had been ambushed by love."

"Yuck."

Granddad chuckled. "You only halfway mean that, Jon, and you know it."

"Yeah, well…"

"I know; old habits die hard. You'll get it one day, same as I did. It starts with infatuation, obsession, like. It cools later, which is as it should be.

"But at first, she'll be all you can think about. You'll see her lovely face when you close your eyes. You'll imagine talking to her, and of course that'll be nothing compared to what happens when she's actually in the room with you."

"I won't be that way."

"You will; don't lie."

"Well, I don't wanna be that way."

"But you do, Jon. You can feel it coming for you. When a girl grabs your attention for the first time, you'll feel as if someone stabbed you in the heart, only it'll be the most delicious pain you've ever felt. You will revel in it. You'll write poetry, you'll sing songs, you'll paint pictures, and none of it will be foolishness if you do it for the right girl." He cleared his throat. "But I'm getting ahead of myself."

"I don't want to hear any more," I said.

He shrugged. "Too bad. You called it out of me, and now you dare not do anything but sit and listen to your elder wax nostalgic. Don't worry, though. It's a good story."

"Does it have guns and adventures in it?" I asked, hoping I'd stumped him. I stood up, pretending to go.

"It sure as hell might; now sit your ass back down and listen to your granddad tell you the story you've been chippin' away at me to hear." He had raised his voice.

I sat immediately.

He cleared his throat again and resumed, calmer. "What I'm about to tell you is important, Jon. I've not told this story to anyone ever before."

I couldn't believe it. "Not even Momma?"

Sadness flashed over his face. "There's history you don't know about, boy. So many things happened that shouldn't have."

This last was an accusation, a gunshot, and it held my life in a balance offset by the chance decisions of others. People like the Leonard. What if my momma had never met him? *I wouldn't have existed. That might have been better. Would it?*

Granddad perceived my sudden grief and reached across the little table to touch my forearm. "I don't mean that the way you're takin' it, son."

"You wish I weren't around?"

"Not at all." He sighed, glancing out the windows toward the meadow rolling down and away below. "No, it's not you I'm angry at. And I'm not angry at Momma," he said, making sure I understood.

"You're angry at my father."

"The Leonard?" he scoffed. "No, son. Not him. I'm angry at me."

"But why?"

"Oh…son, when you live to be my age…no. Wait a while. That's not what I'm trying to say."

"What."

"I was going to say that old men have their regrets, but that's not quite true, is it?"

I shrugged. Was I an old man? I sometimes felt like it. But what did I know.

"What I mean to say is, seventy-five years is a long time, and a man can build up quite a collection of mistakes in that many years. So yes, I have mine.

"You and your momma aren't what I'd call regrets. You're what I'd call treasures. But I've made a lot of mistakes as concerns me." He touched his chest. "A man can hurt people without meaning to, without even trying."

"What, on accident?"

"Son, it happens all the time. You'll see."

Chapter 32

Jonathan

We hadn't left the kitchen table since lunch, and it was already creeping toward suppertime.

"Now," Granddad said, "since I've given you the setup, I can tell you about the day I met Alice Benjamin.

"As these kinds of stories usually go, it was a day that began like any other—at first. It had been a couple of weeks since I'd seen her photograph, and I was beginning to doubt she was a real person."

"Why?"

"Because it wasn't possible that there could be a girl in the world who was that beautiful—and if she were, she would have to be defective in some other way."

"How?"

"Oh, maybe she would have a strident voice. Maybe she stunk. I dunno."

"Oh."

"Anyway, I thought I'd managed to put her out of my mind. I'd finally started to dream and think about boy things again, and I was riding the Mud Cub for the simple enjoyment of it. I would stalk through the woods and spend whole days at the old cabin my ancestors had built. I couldn't spend my energy on a dadgum photograph anyway. And besides, what if she was horrible in person?"

I stayed quiet. I listened.

He waggled a finger. "But I was soon disabused of my folly. One day, well after lunch, in Mr. Benjamin's tired time of the day—something I know all about now but couldn't really understand then—an automobile came up the drive in a cloud of dust.

"When it stopped, two ladies sprang from it. They didn't reach the front porch of the house before they were met by family in a riotous knot sweeping from the house to give them hugs and kisses. Mr.

Benjamin, too, dropped his tools and went running, saying, 'I'll be right back.'

"But he wasn't.

"I continued working, making sure I was oriented in such a way as to see who precisely had come home. *It has to be Alice*, I thought. She'd be coming home with her Aunt Tilda from their trip out west. But from a distance, I couldn't know for certain.

"Eventually the bags were unloaded, everyone went inside, and the car and its driver departed. I assumed I'd been forgotten, but I kept on working because, well, there was work to be done. And also because I wanted a chance to see her in person. I wanted one chance. Just one.

"I had knelt working at a section of wall Mr. Benjamin and I had begun framing. See, you build walls lying flat, and when they're ready, then you stand them up. Destiny crashed into me with a polite cough that came from behind me. 'Hello,' said a voice.

"I turned without standing. And there she was. The girl from the photograph. There was no mistaking her. I stood to my feet and faced her. She was not wearing a dress but had changed into jeans and a work shirt. Her hair was long and straight, pulled back into a loose ponytail like fine cords of amber honey, spun gold in the lowering light, and her eyes stabbed right into me. They were clear, fast pools in a crisp, clean river on a summer morning, complex tones of blue-green turquoise, and alive.

"She said, 'My name is Alice.'

"'I know,' I said, and regretted it right away.

"I could tell she hadn't expected me to say that. I wasn't sure why she'd come to the job site, but now I had derailed any chance of knowing her purpose in saying hello to me. 'Oh?' she said. 'You know my name? How?'

"'I saw your photograph once.' I tried to pull myself away from those eyes, but she had ensnared me completely.

"'Really? When?'

"'At your mother's tea party.'

"'You *are* an interesting boy. And here I thought I was going to come out here merely to be polite and tell you that Mother invited you in for supper.'

"'Oh?'

"'Yes. But now I want to hear more about all this spying on me you've done.'

"'I wasn't spying. I promise. There were some girls making a fuss over your photograph, and I was curious, that's all.'

"She walked away from me through the rough-sawn timber frame I'd been building, glancing back at me over her shoulder. 'And what did they say about me?'

"'They said, 'She's so beautiful.'

"Alice smiled, which nearly knocked me down. Everything about her —from the lightest freckledust across her nose and cheeks, to the way she spoke, to the sound of her voice, to the way her gaze bathed me in her special fire—was bewitching. I couldn't speak. She said, 'And what is your opinion?'

"I had to clear my throat. 'I think,' I said, 'the photograph is very good. Very, very good.' I didn't want to tell her that I had been haunted by it for nearly three weeks and had only begun to recover—and that since we'd met in the flesh not sixty seconds ago, I had begun to lose all hope for life as I'd planned it. Dadgummit, I was ruined for the ordinary; there would never again be any other woman besides her. But I didn't tell her any of that.

"'Oh, stop it,' she said, 'don't tell me about my picture.' She wore a cunning smile. 'I'm standing right in front of you, and you don't even have the decency to tell me *your* name.' I had forgotten to introduce myself. I never do that. And she was flirting with me. With me! I couldn't believe it.

"I held out my hand. 'Malachi Green,' I said.

"She took my hand and was about to say something, but I bent and kissed her ever so softly on her wrist, the way a gentleman in Paris might do. I don't know what came over me, even to this day. She blushed, but I could tell she liked it.

"'Then there was another voice, one I didn't recognize. 'Who's this?'

"'Alice turned. 'Oh, hello, Aunt. I'd like you to meet Malachi Green,' she said.

"'How d'you do,' I said, bowing. Having been caught kissing the hand of the fair maiden, I couldn't break with chivalry now.

"'My, my,' Tilda said, looking at Alice, 'he's a handsome one.' Then she appeared to make up her mind on the spot. 'Alice, dear, you can be as late as you like for supper. I'll tell your parents. It will be fine.' She turned to go, throwing a smirk at Alice as she left.

"This made Alice blush even more. I stood there in her presence, feeling privileged. Privileged, I say."

I broke in, arresting him. "Granddad?"

"Yes, son. What is it?"

I sighed, flustered. "I mean, this is cool, but…"

"Yes?"

"I mean, is that how it happens?"

"What happens."

"Is that how you, I don't know, won her heart? I guess?"

"Jon, a good woman is never won. She must be pursued for life. And sometimes after."

"Oh." I scowled, confused. It sounded to me like a lot of work.

"I will say this," he said. "From that moment on, I was a new person. No other woman could turn my head. Not the way Alice had. She was a goddess."

Chapter 33

Jonathan

Momma called one day to check up on me.

I didn't want to talk to her. I was busy doing man things.

I worried that talking to her would break the beneficent spell Grand-dad had cast over me, worried I'd be pulled back down into the darkness of my childhood.

In a way, that was what happened.

"Hi, sweetie," she said.

I sighed but played it off like I was out of breath from running to the phone. "Hi, Mom."

"How are you doing? I haven't heard a peep from you in weeks. Not even a letter."

"I'm good. Granddad is teaching me a lot."

"Oh, good. I'm glad to hear that. Has he taken you fishing yet?"

"Yes, ma'am. I mean, yeah."

"Catch anything?"

"Yeah. I didn't eat any."

"Mm. It can be tough the first time. I remember when he took me. You have to clean your own fish."

"Yeah. How are *you* doing, Mom? Is everything okay in Chicago?"

"It's sweet of you to ask, honey. Yes, I'm fine. Work is busy-busy-busy. You're familiar. But since you're on your summer break, I don't have much else to do but concentrate on that. Hey—that reminds me. Did you get the packet I sent?"

This irritated me. "Yes, Mom. I read it. What's—I mean, why would I want to go to another summer camp? I have plenty to do around here. I have chores and stuff."

"Honey, I just don't want you to be bored. You know how you get."

"Well, I'm not bored around here. Granddad keeps me busy."

"Oh. Good, sweetie."

"Mom, could you please do me a favor?"

"Yes?"

"Could you not treat me like a kid, please? It's embarrassing when you call me sweetie; I feel like a baby." My cheeks were hot.

"Oh." She fell quiet. "What do you want me to call you, sw—um…"

"Call me Jon, Mom."

Silence. "I can do that." More silence. "Are you sure?"

"Yeah, I'm sure, Mom. I'm ready to start growing up."

There was a sniffle over the line. "My baby."

"I'm not a baby anymore, Mom."

"Well, you'll always be my baby, Jon. Always."

I had the feeling this was the kind of thing mothers said without thinking about it; it gushed out of them whether the moment was right or not. "I know, Ma. Sheesh."

"I love you."

"I love you, too."

She cleared her throat. "So. Tell me something. I need to know so I can sleep better: have you heard anything?"

I knew what she meant without the words spilling naked into the open. When people know each other well, there are certain code languages they use. "No, Momma," I lied.

"Because he's a manipulator."

"I know, Momma. You told me often enough. Besides, I know. From experience."

"Yes." She paused. "I'm only warning you because your father…he took so much from us. For so many years. He will say anything to get to you, sw—uh, Jon. Anything."

"I know, Momma." I felt sorry for her.

"All he wants is somebody's neck to stand on. Anything to make him feel bigger and better. It's how he's wired."

"Momma."

"Yes?"

"I know all that, but I'm safe here."

A sigh. "Yes. Yes, Jon. You are safe at the Forty, aren't you."

I thought, *You're damn right,* but I didn't want her to hear belligerence from me. Not over the phone. She would worry. "Please take care of yourself."

"I will, son."

"Did you want to talk to Granddad?"

"No. No, he's not a big talker on the phone."

He's starting to rub off. "Well, I love you, Momma. Remember that."

"I will. Jon…be a good boy."

"I am."

"Alright."

"And no summer camp, right, Mom?"

"No." She sighed, then continued after a moment. "No, you're right. You're in good hands. I don't know what I was thinking."

"Okay. Remember to lock your doors when you drive, Momma. Granddad tells me Oak Lawn isn't what it used to be, and don't even get me started on Washington Heights."

She laughed. "I don't believe this. Alright, Jon. You behave yourself." More laughter.

"I am."

"I'll call again soon. Love you."

"You too, Ma."

"Goodbye."

"Bye, Momma."

Chapter 34

Jonathan

All this Alice stuff: I didn't know Granddad was capable of mush. I was equal parts enthralled and revolted; I didn't know how to think or what to do. If this was what awaited me in life, I wasn't thrilled.

Sure, I'd noticed girls before. They were weird. Creatures that stirred curiosity but only in a way that asked unanswerable questions. Questions like, *Why is she acting that way around me?* I couldn't supply answers for those kinds of things.

I preferred a good book.

Ella Fitzgerald expressed better how I felt. Granddad loved her music and would stack those records on his hi-fi five high on rainy days. She sang songs without words sometimes: "Baba-doo-zeb." Granddad said it was called scat. I didn't call it that in my head. I called it a siren song because I thought it was beautiful in an inexplicable way. And because it drew me.

That was my kind of living.

Granddad's music opened portals to the past the same way those old photographs in the cardboard box had in the shop. My questions led away from their impacts: spider webs in shards of smashed glass, and each time I gained an insight, there were a hundred more questions without answers leading into the unknown.

I would learn soon enough that life was a constant push into the discomfort of the unknown. I could either look at it with a mind in denial at the frustration it produced or throw up my hands and surrender to the possibilities.

At least it wouldn't be boring.

About girls, though: I was homeschooled, but that didn't mean I hadn't noticed the way a girl could walk. Some of them rolled onto their toes early in every step they took, looking anxious. Others pointed their toes in a little bit. Others didn't walk so much as sway, even swagger.

I didn't consider myself to be all that special, but I did notice how some of them seemed to make a connection with me. It happened at the eyes. Through the eyes. Some of these girls would smile and blush and stand a certain way. Others were more of a riddle. They would come off brusque or flustered. That I didn't get at all.

Sometimes I would lie in front of the hi-fi, propped up on my elbows, peering into the speakers, trying to understand the whole thing through Ella's singing.

Other times I would take the Mud Cub for a ride or stick my nose in a sci-fi comic and try to be transported. Granddad had stacks of those in boxes in the attic.

But the girl thing wouldn't leave me alone. I was drawn to it almost against my will.

I thought of sirens.

Chapter 35

Jonathan

Rain in July.

Midmorning.

Chores done.

And curious again.

"Okay, Granddad," I said, "I need to know what happened next."
I might have come off bossy.

He gave me a look.

We were manning the chairs in the living room, it was the bridge of
a ship, and he was the captain—embroidered anchor on his white hat and
blazing briar pipe sticking out of his mouth. I was the first mate, and the
rain that pelted the windows was spray from a heaving sea.

"What do you want to know now, boy?"

The rain came down, roaring through the gutters, and surely,
I thought, it laid the grass out flat at the ends of the downspouts.

"I want to hear what happened next with Grandma Alice." I didn't
look him in the eyes. "And no mush."

"Mush!" he said, and I could tell he was put off. He set his
newspaper aside, letting it sigh closed along the folds as he gathered up
his pouch of Red Man and took a pinch.

I hid behind my book.

My captain was gruff. "Not every boy falls for an older woman. She
was thirteen. I was only eleven. At those ages, we might as well have been
from different planets."

The storm became a meteor shower. Our ship was now on a mission
to Mars, and the roar at the downspouts became flame that blasted from
our rocket nozzles.

"But we were connected by far more than puppy love," he continued.
"It was a mutual fascination. You have a best friend?"

I was tempted to waggle my book at him as the answer to his question. I couldn't, though. Another void in my life. *Please help me become normal, Granddad. Show me what I'm missing.* "I don't, sir."

His face showed traces of concern and surprise for a split second. "You will. I wouldn't worry." He took up his little brass spittoon. "You're young yet." He spat, the sound wet.

"How can I have a best friend when I'm homeschooled? When will I meet somebody?"

He spat once more. "I dunno. Join 4-H?"

"What's that?"

"Dear God, boy, do you and your momma live under a rock? Never mind." He waved his hands. "As I said, you're young yet. I wouldn't worry." He settled himself into his chair, wriggling his hind end deeper into the stuffing by pushing his hands forward on the broad armrests. "You wanted more of the story."

I closed my book, noticing but not caring that I'd forgotten to stick a bookmark in it. I put it on the side table.

"First, you need to understand that Alice and I were going to be best friends. That kind of thing isn't instant. But it is irresistible. If you don't get that, let me tell you, this story won't make too much sense. You've gotta look at it the right way, Charley."

Thunder cracked outside.

And I couldn't have been happier.

Chapter 36

Jonathan

I wriggled my hind end deeper into the chair, pushing my hands forward on the armrests.

And I listened.

Granddad said, "Mr. Benjamin's barn got built way too fast after me 'n Alice met. I could tell that I wasn't the only one who felt sad about it, too: Mr. and Mrs. Benjamin had taken a liking to me. I had demonstrated that I was both a hard worker and a fast learner; I was eager about life.

"But the job ended; goodbye was inevitable. We parted with a firm handshake, Mr. Benjamin and I, and he told me that he would call me first if he needed more work done around his spread. I thanked him, swung a leg over the Mud Cub, and pedaled the ten miles home.

"It was an early end to the day; it wasn't two in the afternoon yet. I wasn't hungry, so I didn't go home. I didn't want to be there, and anyway, I didn't have to be. I was becoming my own man. My chores were always done before the sun was up so that I could go work and get paid. If there was no work, I could do as I pleased—and not get paid.

"That day, it was my pleasure to kick around in the woods. I had a lot to think about anyhow. Alice hadn't been around when Mr. Benjamin released me. I thought I knew her well enough by then to guess why: she was upset I was leaving.

"But I was wrong. She was busy that morning with her mother, and in her mind, I wasn't shipping out. I'd be around, so there was no need for painful goodbyes. She demonstrated as much when she found me hours later by the old cabin.

"'How'd you find me?' I asked.

"Her lips were parted, revealing just one slightly irregular tooth. God, she was beautiful. She pointed to the Mud Cub lazing on his side in the leaves nearby. Her face was pure and honest. 'You're not hard to find,' she said.

"'What's that supposed to mean?' I asked.

"She gasped. 'You thought mean things about me, I can tell.'

"'What? How can you say that?'

"She punched me in the arm pretty hard. She was wearing jeans and a t-shirt, and she reached back and pulled the tie out of her hair. It spilled down over her shoulders. It made me crazy to behold her standing there in all her glory. 'I can say that,' she said, 'because it's obvious you thought you were never going to see me again.'

"I thought about it for a second. 'Well,' I countered, 'can you blame me? The barn's finished, and you didn't bother to say goodbye to me.'

"She combed her hair out with her fingers. 'That's because I didn't have any goodbyes to say, Malachi Green. I was planning on coming around later.'

"'Well, what were you doing all morning?'

"She gathered her hair together and pulled it back again, tighter than before, her perfect face gilded in the leafy sunlight that filtered through boughs high above us. 'Girl stuff. I came around, didn't I?'

"'Yeah, you did.' I play-punched her in the shoulder.

"'Weak.'

"She had three older brothers, two of whom were out of the house and on their own. The other was away at boarding school. 'Do you want me to hit you harder?' I asked.

"'No. I can tell that you missed me. And it's all I need.' She turned and picked up the Mud Cub and swung a leg over. 'So, Mr. Green. What's on the agenda for today?'

"Standing there astride my bicycle at thirteen years old, she was becoming a woman already. I decided I would chase her. 'I don't want to do anything but hang around with you,' I said. 'I'm content to throw rocks into the creek, just as long as we're together.'

"She belly laughed; it was magic. 'My father worries.'

"'About what?'

"'About you, Mr. Green.'

"'Yeah? Why?'

"'Because you're a handsome young man with a strong voice.'

"I came closer, standing over the front wheel, steadying the bike by holding onto the bars as I faced her. She was even more beautiful close up. She placed her feet on the pedals, and I balanced her there. 'And why should Mr. Benjamin worry about little ol' me?' I asked.

"'Because you're dangerous, Malachi Green, and we Benjamins all know it.'

"'Yeah? How?' I came closer to her, leaning in, drawn nearer by her gravity.

"'Oh, I don't know,' she said, her eyelids relaxing as she sighed. 'You're a hard worker. You're ambitious.'

"'And that makes me dangerous.'

"'Oh, yes, Mr. Green. Very.'

"Our faces were inches apart. Her breath was sweet cream. I said, 'You'd better look out, Alice.' I closed my eyes and leaned forward to kiss her.

"I was only going to give her a peck on the cheek, mind you. But as I shifted my weight, I upset the apple cart. I forgot we were balanced. We both tumbled to the ground in a clumsy heap, tangled up in each other and the bicycle.

"'What just happened?' she laughed. 'The ground reached up and bit us.'

"I was too embarrassed to be embarrassed. I laughed and tried to get untangled from her and the bicycle. I helped her up and said, 'Come on. Let's go throw rocks.' We left the Mud Cub where he lay."

Chapter 37

Jonathan

"You left the Mud Cub just sitting there?" I asked.

"I was, eh…transported, you might say," he said. "Alice and I threw rocks in that creek until we changed how the water flowed through it and the banks were nude. The sun was low, so we decided to call it a day.

"I walked her home, and there at the end of her daddy's drive by the mailbox, I finally got to kiss her. On the cheek. And I watched for a moment as she walked homeward. My lips tingled from that contact for hours.

"I was so lost about it, I was under the covers that night before I realized I'd left the Mud Cub out in the woods. I felt bad, but that was where he would have to spend the night. I'd found something that mattered more.

"You see what was happening. I was around the bend for her. And what made me surer was that I knew she was around the bend for me."

I interrupted. "Granddad?"

"Yes, Jon."

"Is that like being over the hill?"

All expression fled from his face. "You know, for such a smart kid, you're sure clueless about this stuff."

"What?" I was defensive.

"Never mind. Wait a while. Where was I?"

"You were around the bend." His eye caught my own, and I averted. "Sir," I added, but that seemed like it didn't help.

"I was telling you how I fell in love with your grandmother. Reminiscin' like."

"Yes, sir." I took a pinch of Big League Chew from my pouch and tucked it into my cheek, sucking on it, pretending it was tobacco. The storm outside said, *Come on, come on, shh, crack, boom.* My ears flexed and opened, hearing more.

Granddad started up again. "Alright. Breakfast with my father one morning a few weeks later, I guess it was. We sat and talked about Alice Benjamin. He was a man of few words, Jon. Like you."

My heart skipped a beat.

"He asked me about her. That meant he had taken notice; he cared about both me and her. And I told him that I thought I loved her. He was quiet for a long time. Then he nodded and took a bite of his eggs. Then he said something I'll never forget."

"What was it, Granddad?"

"He said, 'You're doing a fine job, son.' I took that statement to be his endorsement. He had given me my wings, Jon."

I took a moment to think all this through. Granddad had fallen quiet. After a while I asked, "What happened next?"

"Wait a while; let me think. It was raining that day. Like it is today." He gestured toward the windows of our ship. The wind topped a wave. Cascades of salt spray whitecapped onto the glass, and I regarded my captain.

"I wanted to go see Alice more than anything. My father's blessing was a thing I could carry with me in my hip pocket, ready to produce at a challenge. I was in possession of bucketloads of goodwill, not only from him but from the Benjamins, not the least formidable of whom was Tilda. That's how you're sure, boy; it's at least one way, when you find her."

"What, about being around the bend?"

"No, son, about whether you've found a good woman and whether you're worthy enough to pursue her." He waved his arms. "There will be bucketloads of goodwill coming for you from every good person in her universe. Some evil people, some selfish people, won't give you their endorsement. But those whose endorsement matters most will smile on you. And if you're pursuing a woman, you'll need all the encouragement you can find."

"I'm confused."

He grabbed his spittoon. "I bet." He spat and set it back down. "But you'll remember my words when you need 'em. Meanwhile, the story. You want to hear more, right?"

"Yes, sir."

"I wanted to see her. I swung a leg over the Mud Cub and took off through the storm. You remember how I was saying Alice took the Mud Cub's place in my life, how he had to let me go?"

"Yes, sir."

"Mm-hm. Well, he didn't let me go without a fight. I was about a mile from here when he threw his chain. Popped right off the chainring and jammed between the chainguard and chainring. It locked up and about threw me off."

"Did you hit a big bump?"

"Good, kid. No. You would think I had, but the road was smooth and sticky; the rain had taken all the sharp edges off everything. The Mud Cub was throwing a fit. I tell you that bicycle is something special.

"When I stopped, I managed to get my fingers in under the guard and remount the chain on the top side of the chainring. After that, it was as simple as giving the crank a rotation and letting the rear wheel spin until the chain was back on track; everything sucked right back into line."

"And he was okay?"

"No worse for the wear. But he wasn't done yet. The chain came off a second time in less than a mile. This time, if he'd been a horse, I'd have wanted to beat him. But I remounted the chain and carried on. Now I was soaked and filthy, and I carried on more because of sheer stubbornness. I knew that if I knocked on Alice Benjamin's door dressed in mud and desperation, they would think something terrible had happened to me or my father, but I kept on going. The Mud Cub punished me for it. I was five miles from home when the rear tire gave out."

"Oh, no."

"A flat tire was a death knell."

"What did you do then?"

Granddad chuckled. "The only thing I could do. I gave up."

"Wait. You gave up?"

"Yeah, Jon. Only a fool keeps going for the sake of his pride. Nothing good can come after that point if you keep going. I stuck a shoulder through the frame and carried him home in the rain. Five miles. The Mud Cub and I said goodbye on that long walk, as I carried my fighter back to garrison. In those weary five miles, my heart suffered a change. The Mud Cub lost his glow, and I could see he was just a machine, not a dreammaker. You know the saying about hindsight being twenty-twenty?"

"Yes, sir. It means you see something clearer after you go through it."

"Right. Walls appearing to be huge become anthills once we step over them. I would have thought you were crazy if you'd have told me the Mud Cub was going to be an ephemeron, but he was."

"What's an ephemeron?"

"Eh…It's like a flash in the pan."

"Oh."

"The Mud Cub was a tool that would affect my trajectory, but he wasn't a thing I could build my life around. Son, so much about life is momentary and light, whether it's hardship or ecstasy. You can find joy in both if you suck the marrow right out of each moment."

I scowled. "What do you mean, Granddad?"

"I mean joy isn't just a feeling of happiness. That's what I mean."

I decided to stop asking questions.

"Did you know some insects only live for a day once they finally get their wings?"

I didn't, but I didn't say as much with words.

"That's an ephemeron."

"So you abandoned him for Alice?"

Granddad grunted and spat. "More like he abandoned me, don't you think?"

I thought. "I guess," I said, but that didn't mean I agreed. I wanted to defend the bicycle's honor, but I saw right away how foolish it would be to try. Alice was my own grandmother. And I was sitting here in her chair. I wondered what conversations had sallied forth between these two chairs when she'd been around.

"Truth is," Granddad said, "there comes a time in every boy's life when he has a choice to make; a Big Choice."

He leaned toward me over the side table between us.

"There comes a time when a boy has to put off his childishness and begin his journey to maturity. To manhood. This choice will determine whether or not he's going to be a real man or a wraith."

I felt pinned. But I took it. I wanted it.

And then, like destiny, there came a knock at the front door.

Granddad was up in a flash. He was so fast that it felt like time had slowed for me. My ears and cheeks were on fire. I knew who it was. I heard the rain become louder as the door swung open, but I didn't dare look.

"Well, now," Granddad said. "If the devil don't appear when he hears his name."

Chapter 38

Jonathan

The Leonard was here.

I was more scared than I'd ever been.

"Hello, Malachi." I could feel him probing for me. "Where's my son?"

"How dare you, you son of a bitch."

My ears were ringing; I ran away quick, toward the back of the house, and I heard Granddad say with calm control, "I want nothing more than to kill you right where you stand." I burst through the door to the mudroom and dove under a shelf and hid.

I heard shouting. There were some chapter-and-verse biblical quotations; the Leonard's voice scraped over the floorboards, slithering toward me here under the shelf, sniffing for me.

"I have a right to see my son," I heard.

My hands flashed toward my ears, covering them tight. I squeezed my eyes shut. I could hear muffled arguments skimming over the top of my breathing, raked raw.

A gun went off. It came through my covered ears as a harsh pop, but it was unmistakable.

The front door slammed and locked. I heard heavy footfalls in the living room. Granddad's voice: "Jon? Where are you, son?"

This was unlike I'd ever heard him. His voice left no room for debate or doubt. It was pure command and control.

I heard the sound of the slide being racked on the twelve-gauge. "Jon? Are you in the house?" Heavy footfalls raced up the stairs.

I remained hiding.

The back doorknob rattled. I gasped and peeked out. I saw the Leonard's face there in the lowest pane. His eyes widened when he saw me. There was a pistol in his hand that he hid as soon as I saw it.

I ran.

I heard, muffled: "No, Jonathan. Come back." His voice was thin; he kept it low. He didn't want to be heard.

I ran to the kitchen, hearing Granddad's footsteps above moving toward my bedroom. He called out, "Jon, where are you?" I couldn't answer. I hid behind the chairs under the kitchen table trying to breathe, crying dry.

That face appeared at the window over the sink; I could see his black eyes and hear him hissing, "Come on, Jonathan. Let's bust you out of here. Come with me."

I bolted, thwocking my head off the table and overturning chairs. I ran for the staircase. The thunder of Granddad's big size twelves rolled down it, relief on his face, the twelve-gauge cannon in his hands. "Granddad, help," I wheezed through my terror, pointing toward the kitchen.

With a nod, he moved toward the Leonard and brought the shotgun up to his shoulder. "Stay with me, Jon."

I turned and tucked in behind him, keeping small. He addressed my father. "You show your face, I blow a hole right through it."

There was a plaintive protest from right outside the kitchen window: "But he's mine."

I peeked around the side of Granddad's left hip and saw those eyes peeking over the sill. They were angry and hungry. I knew too well the dark, boozy haze they reeked of.

Granddad dropped the hammer. The muzzle blast was immense; the twelve-gauge erupted, belching smokefire. Deafness screamed into my ears and took up all space in the closeness of the room.

A canned scream from outside in the rain, smothered under cotton balls, panicky and flooded with indignation.

We moved through the back door, Granddad quicker than I, and I saw the Leonard with his tail tucked and one hand to his head, running through the pouring rain around toward the front of the house.

He was whimpering, "Jesus! Jesus!" over and over again, and I thought it ironic because I'd never heard him pray, and I'd never seen a hint of reverence on him for anyone but himself.

Granddad pointed the shotgun at the sky. "Cover your ears, Jon." I managed to do so right before he unleashed another blast. The Leonard slipped and fell in reaction to the sound, but he scrambled to his feet again, clutching his little pistol and continuing around the corner toward the front.

Granddad burst back into the house, repeating his command to "Stay with me, Jon." He was quicker than I'd ever seen him move. Through the mudroom, down the hall, past the stairs, I followed—running taller now—and then we busted through the front door, Granddad leading with the muzzle of the twelve-gauge.

The Leonard had reached the opposite side of a car I didn't recognize. In the passenger seat, the side closest to us, I could see the milk-white face of a woman I didn't know, her eyes dumb but bulging with terror.

The Leonard's hands were raised in the rain, and as it washed over his filthy countenance, it looked like tears streamed down and pinked with the blood that ran from a gash over one eye. "I'm going, I'm going." His voice was as thin as newsprint. "I'm going," he said again, but he hesitated.

"Get in the car," Granddad said. "You know I will kill you if you don't."

My father's smile was grease. I had to turn my head away. "But he's mine," he said.

"Cover your ears, Jon." These words were the darkest I'd yet heard. Through my flesh-and-bone muffles, I heard the cannon let go once more.

The shot was aimed high and took out a few small branches in the big sycamore, sending one red squirrel into a panicked fury as everything came down.

Then he took aim at the Leonard, and his voice resounded, "Get off my land!" He stepped into the rain on the walkway, the weapon aimed at the Leonard's face. He repeated the command, only this time seasoned with the mother of all curse words.

The Leonard, finally forced, finally obeyed. He scurried behind the wheel. The door slammed, the engine strained to life, and his car slithered down the drive as if scalded by shame.

Granddad moved forward, chasing away a predator. He fired another shot, this one aimed at the ground behind the fleeing vehicle. He racked the slide, moving farther, taking aim again as the car picked up speed. He fired another. The tortured engine redlined, and as the transmission upshifted, the tires broke loose in our soaked gravel. It was like the car was desperate to get away but highly pissed about how it was being used.

Granddad racked the slide again and took aim, standing supreme at the top of his drive. But then he lowered the muzzle. I could see his shoulders heaving up and down.

He stood in the rain.

I stood far behind on the leading edge of the porch.

He lowered the muzzle, lifted his face to the sky, and—honest to God—he roared. Loud and long and fierce.

After a while he came out of the rain, and we both went inside.

For supper, he baked us a Red Baron pizza in the oven.

Pepperoni.

And then we sat and read books on the bridge of our ship.

Chapter 39

Jonathan

Granddad tucked me into bed that night. It was the only time in his life he did that.

Then he prayed for me. Most of the prayer was, incredibly, a fount of gratitude. He thanked the Good Lord for the rain, for protection, for gunpowder, and for miracles like frozen pizzas. And then he thanked Him for me, praying He would hold me in His right hand all night and "speak comfort" to me.

I'd never heard anything like it.

When he had finished, he said, "You okay, Jon?"

"Yeah," I whispered, and he let it slide. He sighed heavy and brushed the hair from my eyes in the most incredible gesture of tenderness I'd ever felt. I could imagine he'd done the same exact thing for my momma when she was young, when this had been her room.

Then I could not stop the tears from overflowing from within me. All I could manage was, "I'm sorry, Granddad," before I burst into sobs fit to move heaven and earth.

I turned away from him and curled into myself. He patted my back until I had finished, which was a good long time.

Then I was exhausted, and sleep snatched me down until half a second later, when the sun had spread itself over the quilt, making me sticky with sweat: the night had passed me right by.

It had been dreamless.

My eyes wouldn't open at first. They were welded shut with my dried tears. But I wasn't scared now, unlike the first time it had happened.

A new day had begun a while ago, but I drew the covers—though I was hot—over my ears and stared at the room sideways for a while.

But then I got up and went down to breakfast.

"Don't worry about your chores, boy; they're already done."

I nodded and sat down at the table in my usual spot.

"You sleep alright?" he asked.

"Yes, sir," I said, falling silent for a minute or two. "Granddad, have you ever fallen asleep and not dreamed and then woken up where it feels like only a couple of seconds have gone by? But it's a totally new day?"

He smiled. "Yes, Jon. A new day."

"It's weird."

"I agree," he said, and offered me a breakfast of bacon and eggs and pancakes. Unlike a lot of men his age, Granddad could cook things from scratch when he chose to, and his cooking was good.

When I thought about it, I imagined his hand had been forced into these kinds of things when Grandma Alice died. I could see them as a joyful couple, her happy to cook their meals and him happy to provide the raw materials she would use for them, each one a happy part of a whole that was greater than the sum of its parts because they joyfully served each other.

I wondered what made people so confused about what made a man a man and a woman a woman these days, why my mom couldn't have found a halfway decent man, why she worked so hard so we could scrape by, why there was no help for her. And why she couldn't seem to find a counterpart who needed *her* help. What had happened to the world? What had happened to the Green family?

The bacon and eggs were good. Granddad made what he called "froached" eggs. He said it was a cross between fried and poached because he fried them in butter with a glass lid over the skillet, and the steam poached the tops so the whites got cooked all the way through without any need of turning them over.

I enjoyed them, but I thought "froached" sounded too much like roach, which was disgusting when you were sopping up your runny yolks with your pancakes.

"Did I scare you yesterday?" he asked. He lowered his newspaper. "I wanted to wait until you had some food in your belly before we moved on from smalltalking."

"I'm sorry I told him where I'd be—"

"No, no. That's not what I'm getting at. I blame you for nothing, Jon. Do you hear me? For nothing. Are we clear?"

"Yes, sir." There were a few bites left on the plate, and I decided I wanted them, so I began eating again.

"Did I scare you yesterday?"

I thought about this. "Only in a good way."

He grunted. "Well. I'm sorry I lost it afterward. Yellin' that way."

I swallowed. "I thought it was cool," I said. I took another bite.

"Well, now." He appeared to consider this. "And I also apologize for using foul language in front of you, but at some point you're gonna learn it, and you might as well learn it from me."

"I already knew those words, Granddad." I thought he would have known that, but he was an honorable man who thought the best first. His apology was a matter of procedure. And I accepted.

He sighed. "The world ain't what it used to be." He took a sip of his coffee and thought for a moment. "I'll tell you this," he said. "That squirrel's damn lucky."

"Why?" I took my last bite, trying to appear casual and grown-up.

"Because I missed him the first time. And because he was real scarce when I was ready to kill and had run out of targets."

I snorted. "You would have shot him if you saw him?"

Granddad shrugged. "Stew. Or bait," in explanation, then changed the subject. "Listen to me, son. I want you to know this."

I sat up in my chair and braced myself against the table. I had been way out in uncharted territory for a long time, but I still wasn't used to it.

"The Leonard may be your father by blood, but he's just a sperm donor. He's no father, and you don't belong to him anymore." Granddad leaned forward and balled up a fist nice and tight, held it, then set it down on the table carefully. "You're under my protection now."

I nodded, breathing real quiet.

"That creature is not a man. He may look and come off like a man, but he's not. He's a wraith, a devil. He's unworthy of you, Jon."

I nodded, shouting inside, *Please go on. Please.*

"You are to fight creatures like him with everything you have in you. Clear?"

I nodded.

"And *I'm with you,* son. I don't ever want to see you give in or surrender to him or his kind. He is unworthy. You, Jon, are worthy. You are awake. He is not. You are a steward of light and reason. He is possessed by darkness; he is its little whore. You let your light shine and be bold, you hear?" His voice cracked. "You be a son to me, Jon. You be a son to me." A single tear ran down his weathered cheek. "Will you?"

I nodded into the back of my hand. "Yes, sir."

He took off his glasses and wiped his eyes. "Alright then."

A moment passed. I said, "Granddad?"

We were both looking out the kitchen window. Last night I'd helped him nail a section of plywood over the one broken pane, but the sill was still pitted and blasted, naked guts of pine board on display. "Yeah?" he responded.

"May I change my name to Green?"

He was so quiet that I thought he'd died. "Yes. Yes, you may," he said, finally. Then he said, "You're a good boy, Jon Green."

"Thanks, Granddad."

Chapter 40

Jonathan

Days rolled by.

Time covered the rawness of my wounds with its passing.

I busied myself with chores, worrying over the new chick that had hatched. And I wandered the woods, exploring its many rifts and ridges, discovering the little cabin hewn from timber and then raised and roofed by my ancestors.

Granddad headed to town one day, saying he needed to talk to a lawyer about my name change and some other stuff.

I found the creek he and Alice had thrown stones into over sixty years ago. I threw a few stones myself, once I had grappled with my reverence for the place. I decided this was hallowed ground, yes…but it was also my birthright to stand here.

And that was significant.

So I stood there on the bank, and I did what was customary for the Green family: I threw stones into the creek.

A few days later I went to him and said, "Granddad, will you help me set up some targets? I want to learn how to use the Winchester."

"Yeah? And I suppose you also want me to let you fire the revolver?"

"Yes, sir, if it's not too much trouble."

"And would you also like me to make you a sandwich while I'm at it?"

I didn't get it until he pretend-punched my shoulder. Then I said, "Actually, if you're taking orders, a PB and J would be nice."

"Well, I ain't takin' orders. Not from you, boy." He smiled. "I'll help you set up some targets, but you can make your own damn sandwiches." He was already moving toward the corner where the twelve-gauge lived. "Here," he said, "take this one; we'll use it. And I'll get the Winchester, too."

"And the revolver?"

"Yes, little sir."

We set up a firing range in the back yard (a huge meadow comprising at least ten acres) with hay bales and old milk jugs and the woods in front of us.

A card table was our workbench—the three guns laid down on it muzzles away, black and deadly. We were Meriwether Lewis and William Clark, and we were about to barter with Indians over this table.

Granddad was Lewis, of course. I wasn't about to be a man named Meriwether (Granddad was old; it fit him better).

"Granddad, where did you learn so much about guns?"

"I joined the Marine Corps after the crash in twenty-nine. I was seventeen, nearly eighteen. I was line infantry, a ground pounder."

"What's a ground pounder?" I asked.

He took up the Winchester and made sure there weren't any bullets in it. "A regular old-fashioned soldier. Rifles and marching and hand-to-hand combat. And bayonets." He shoved the bolt forward. "It's clear." He handed the rifle to me. "Keep it aimed away from you; muzzle awareness. That's right. Dry fire it a few times and get a feel for where the trigger lets go."

I did. It was light and silky.

"This gun is special," he said.

"So, what happened after you joined? And why did you join up? What happened to Alice?"

"I joined up because the crash of twenty-nine gave birth to a train of years in which a lot of people lost hope. I knew a few trades, but if nobody has any money to hire a carpenter, a carpenter can't work—and if a carpenter can't work, he won't eat. I saw opportunity in the Marine Corps, so I jumped."

He showed me how to cock the rifle by pulling the bolt lever up and back, then forward and back down, and I settled into it again. *Snick.* The trigger let go, and the firing pin protruded into an empty chamber. "But what about Alice? Did you have to leave her behind?" I cocked it again.

"Only in the beginning. She couldn't come with me to boot camp, could she?"

Snick. "I dunno. I guess not."

"I missed her more than anything, and it was tough for us for a while. I trained at the then-brand-new base in San Diego. I was ambitious, Jon. I earned my promotions fast. I became a corporal in only a year, so some of my bosses took notice and recommended me for what would eventually become Marine Force Recon in the fifties. But in the thirties, it wasn't even the Raider Battalion yet."

These were magic words. Their meaning was enshrouded, which made them cool. "What did you do?"

"I trained to be a sniper. My job was to get flown behind enemy lines and drop in via parachute or glider."

"Whoa."

"Here, you're ready for live ammo." He showed me how to load it.

"So, what did you actually do?" I asked.

"Top secret missions. Only a handful of officials knew about it."

Granddad was a badass. This wasn't news.

We donned our earmuffs, and I took aim, squeezing the Winchester's trigger the way he'd taught me. My first shot obliterated a milk jug and nearly bowled me over. I pulled my cheek up from the stock to look at the effects.

"Not bad, Jon." He slapped me on the shoulder. "Powerful weapon, uh?"

"Damn," was all I could say. It made him laugh.

Then there were more Alice stories. I had to confess I was starting to get it about how he loved her, how they could be best buddies though they were boy and girl, man and woman.

He told me how the wedding had been small, plain by today's standards, and how they were married in an old church building long since demolished. His father was his best man the day Alice Benjamin became Alice Green. "She was the most beautiful girl in the whole wide world. And who would have thought," he said, "Helen of Troy only lived ten miles from here."

She was twenty, he was eighteen, already a Marine corporal, and it was 1930. They wanted a big, huge family, but something was wrong. They couldn't have children for some reason, no matter how bad they wanted to. But I didn't want to know any more about that. I asked about other stuff, cool stuff.

Granddad went to school and earned his degree in engineering from Cal Poly in 1937, being accepted to Marine Officer Candidate School the same year. He received his first command—an infantry platoon—in 1938 and made captain in 1939.

That was the year he bought the Cadillac. For Alice.

Sarah, my momma, didn't come along until 1952, when Granddad was forty, and when she did, they were both so thrilled that they called her a miracle baby.

And then his daddy died in 1954.

"Time for the pistol?" he asked me.

I nodded.

"Now, this is going to be different, son. Pistols are close-range weapons." He showed me how it worked, then we walked toward the remaining milk jugs, up close and personal with the targets.

"Wow," I said, "with a pistol you're really close to what you're shooting at."

"Yep," he said. "Changes things, doesn't it?"

"Yes, sir."

"This is the biggest handgun they make. It's a one-shot-one-kill weapon, provided you hit your target. There are others—the .357 and the Derringer, which is just a little pop gun with two bullets, but again, either of those can kill a man."

"This one makes a bigger hole?"

"Hoo-ee. Think you could take down a deer with a revolver?"

"I don't know. Can a revolver do that?"

"This one can. You heard of the *Dirty Harry* movie?"

"Yes, sir."

"This is the gun: a .44 magnum. It's no nonsense."

He was right. It was heavy. It kicked so hard I scraped the bridge of my nose with the hammer spur on my first shot. "I love this thing."

"See what it did?" He pointed.

The milk jug had been cauliflowered; ripples of plastic opened wide where the bullet had ripped through.

"A .44 magnum bullet will go through damn near anything, Jon. Walls. Doors. Men. If you find you ever need it, I keep it in my nightstand drawer."

I took this information in, but my mind was elsewhere. I wasn't sure how to phrase my question, so I blurted it out. I think it was better this way. "Granddad?"

"Yes, Jon."

"How did she die?"

I had shocked him. He bit his lips down tight and took a minute. "My Alice started getting sick in nineteen sixty-one. She was in a great deal of pain; she—well, there was a lot to it.

"She lingered with me for almost two years. It was my honor and privilege to care for her. To shelter her.

"She died after a series of strokes in sixty-three. About this time of year."

I was afraid to move.

"You be careful cleaning this up," he said as he turned and walked into the house.

Part 5: Granddad

Chapter 41

Malachi

I got two pieces of mail with the lawyer's letterhead on them.

One of them was for me; it would go into the safe along with the insurance papers. All the other stuff—the details—I buried deep in the hoard in the carriage house. I supposed he would find it one day when the Good Lord decided he was ready for it. Would I be around to see it? Would it matter if I were? Probably not, to both.

The second piece of mail was for Jon, so after I opened it and read what it said, I called him.

He came into the kitchen no longer citified and soft but savage and bronzed, the light of understanding stout and afire upon the torch of his soul. "Yes, sir?"

"Letter came for you." I chucked it across the table and stood up. "Coffee?" It was late morning.

"Yes, sir," he said, glancing at the cover letter. He pulled out his customary chair and sat, reading.

I poured his cup and set it in front of him. "Well?" I said. "What do you think?"

"Jonathan Green. It's official."

"Yep," I sipped from my own cup. "Pretty 'cool,' I guess you would say."

"Thanks, Granddad. You don't know how much this means."

"Yes, I do. And you're more than welcome."

We both fell quiet for a while. Then I added, "What you name a thing matters a great deal. You'll call it by that name hundreds of thousands of times. And if it matters for things, it matters even more for people. You know what your name means, Jon?"

"No, sir."

"It means 'gift of God.'" He didn't have anything to say to this, but I saw what it did to him. "And now you're home. You're a Green. I want to make it clear to you that you have a father now."

He nodded but said nothing. I figured he was searching for the right words, as was his custom. That was fine with me.

"Come on, son. Bring your paper with you." We walked out onto the front porch, where I'd set up the camera on a tripod.

"Stand over there and hold your letter." I composed the image I wanted and focused it, leaving space for me to stand beside him. I set the timer, and soon we had a fresh snap of a one-time orphan and an old widower beaming about the newness of life that is only found in the ordinary things.

Just a moment captured. A tick of the inexorable clock.

But it was all right there on film. I would develop this roll and have them make a print for each of us.

We stuck his official name change document in a frame and hung it in a place of honor over the fireplace with my Marine Corps warrants. My old brag sheets had good company then.

As the day wore on, Jon busied himself outside.

I figured maybe he was out defending the cabin against invaders, using the Mud Cub to put down long, dark skids in the fresh chipseal on County Line Road, or maybe floating a fleet of sticks down the creek.

He was doing things a boy ought to be doing, in other words.

I was glad of it. Glad, I say, and for the first time in a long while.

I meant what I'd told the boy about his name. I really did see him as a gift from God.

I'd been in danger of dimming down into bitter embers, an old man lonely and full of resentment for a world that was leaving him behind.

But Jon had stoked my fire. And I was ablaze once more.

Part 6: Jon

Chapter 42

Jon

There was no mistaking it for a nightmare; it was too real. I woke, startled, to the demonic face of the Leonard.

I pushed back, away from him—but he had my head in a vise, one hand clamped over my mouth and the other behind my head. His eyes were black and hooded. He was shushing me and whispering for me to be quiet. "It's okay. Daddy's here."

He wore nothing but sweatpants and a pair of socks. As my reason began to take hold, I thought he'd needed to take off his shoes in order to creep into the house unnoticed, but his shirt?

"How did you get in here?" I said, but it was like trying to speak in a dream. My voice was muffled under his hand.

"Jonathan, sweetheart, it's Daddy. I'm here now. Shh."

I calmed my body. I hoped he would take his salty hand from over my mouth.

"Will you be quiet?"

Words like daggers in my heart. He'd said exactly these many times before, most recently just after he'd broken two of my ribs. But I nodded.

He removed his hands, wiping them on his thighs.

"Listen," he whispered. "I'm here to break you out, buddy. Come on, let's go."

"I don't want to go anywhere with you."

"Come on, champ. We've got toys for you in the car; it's down the road."

"No."

"Jonathan. The old man has been poisoning your mind, making you believe in fairy tales. But I'm real. I'm here. I had a lot of things I needed to take care of, and I'm sorry I wasn't around for a while, but I'm here now. Daddy wants to take care of you again. I've really missed you." He held his hands up in a posture of surrender, but they were more like a trap ready to be sprung. "Come on," he whispered. "I've risked a lot just coming. Let's get you out of here."

"No."

"Come on, Jonathan. Let's go. Someone's in the car; she's waiting."

"Who?" I asked, raising my voice.

His hand snapped over my mouth once more. "Shh," he hissed, livid. "It's a surprise. She's excited to meet you. Let's go."

He pulled me out of my bed too quickly for me to find anything to anchor to. The Leonard wasn't big, but he was strong. He pulled me toward him and wrapped me up facing away from him, tight to his chest, one hand over my mouth, the other pinning my arms. My feet were free, so I kicked with them, but they caught only dead air.

He twisted me away from the bed and began walking me toward the bedroom door and the stairs, shushing into my ear the whole time, saying, "Daddy's here; let's go."

I was frantic, searching for something to kick against, but it was dark and the shadows were thick. I would have tried to bite his hand, but it was too tight over my lips, so I sucked in as much air as I could through my nose and screamed into his fingers, still flailing my legs. My foot finally connected with the tin trash can. When it came down across the room, it was like a gunshot in the quiet dark.

The Leonard cursed. He suspended my whole body now by my head with the hand that muzzled me. His other hand came free and reached down toward my privates and squeezed hard. It hurt bad, and I cried out.

The hall light came on.

I heard Granddad coming.

"Look what you did," the Leonard said, his breath caustic in my ear.

The doorway opened, and Granddad appeared in it, backlit, his face carrying deep shadows in the yellow light. He saw. "Oh, *hell* no," he said.

"I'll hurt him," the Leonard yelled, his voice grating. "You let us go, or I'll hurt him."

Granddad stopped. "No."

"He's mine. I'm taking him back."

"You'll do no such thing. He's not going with you. Put him down."

"I'll hurt him!"

"No," Granddad said again. I was struggling for air; my nostrils flared. "Jon's not your son anymore."

"Bullshit!"

The smell pouring off the Leonard was making me gag. I wanted to be free of him more than anything I'd ever wanted before. What could I do, though? I was smaller than him; I was fully bound by his grasp.

But I hoped in my struggle, and I did manage to get one hand free.

I reached down quickly for *his* groin, and I twisted and crushed as hard as I could.

He cried out. His grip on me failed. I dug an elbow into his ribs and pulled further away as he went down.

"Damn you!" he shrieked at me.

I scrambled toward Granddad, who was closing the distance. His face was the picture of vengeance. He swung his left hand downward, seizing the Leonard by the throat and picking him straight up, holding him high like a fish on a stringer. Granddad cocked his right fist.

The Leonard was frightened, but there was sick victory in his bulging eyes as he hung there. His right hand descended to his waistband, to a greasy spot at the small of his back. When it came around into the light, I could see a little pistol.

Before I could say or do anything, it had gone off, and both men collapsed together in a heap on the floor.

I felt small. I could think of only one thing: the top drawer of Granddad's nightstand.

Chapter 43

Jon

I already knew what it felt like to flee. The mind outruns the body, but the body doesn't respond the way it should, which makes everything worse.

The mind freaks out and you become trapped inside yourself, the mind an unwilling captive in a tomb of flesh and bone. The connection between them goes dumb. Limbs become clumsy.

I struggled as fast as I could toward Granddad's bedroom, the threat of the Leonard's malevolence draped over me unseen from behind, a touchless cloak of darkness scrambling after me.

Tripping down the hall, landing on all fours, the runner bunching up under my flailings, through the door running mostly upright, hand on switch, light coming on, daring to plunge ahead and not look back, on two feet now, seeing the nightstand, thinking prayers in lightning, *God, let it be there,* and hoping the Leonard wasn't right on my heels as I crashed to my knees, stupid ungrasping hands pawing at the handle of the drawer, sliding it open, and there:

The .44.

"God Almighty." This was my invocation.

The instant my hand touched the gun, I heard a second shot. I pulled my hand back as if I'd been electrocuted.

No—the shot had come from my bedroom.

I snatched up the .44 with both hands, the strength of my arms so sucked out I had difficulty raising the weapon, but I turned around and held the heavy thing, pushing up against its push back down.

"Granddad?" There was no answer, and my voice reminded me of things I had been trying to avoid my whole life. I stood at his bedroom doorway, but I wasn't close enough to see what was going on.

I heard a muffled voice, then shuffling in the hall.

I cocked the hammer.

Something crashed in the stairwell. A picture frame?

Noises from downstairs.

I made my way into the hall.

There was blood on the floor; a splatter. And a fingerprint farther along, on the wall near the banister at the top of the stairs. I picked up my pace.

When I gained the doorway to my bedroom, I saw Granddad lying on his back. Right there on my floor, right over the holes I'd made with the shotgun when I was just a boy trying to be a man and didn't know anything of it. There was a little pistol beside him on the floor.

Granddad had taken a bullet in the chest. He was struggling.

The Leonard wasn't here.

I cast aside the .44 on top of the dresser.

I knelt at Granddad's side.

"Jon," he said, "he's going to try to kill you." There was blood on his shirt, more blood than I'd ever seen. "Had a Derringer on him. He went downstairs, son. I managed to injure him with it." His voice was wet.

Managed to injure him.

That was the second shot. The first had done what I was looking at here.

He held up his right hand and made a weak V with two fingers. "Two things." He was short of breath. "Phone in my bedroom. Call nine-one-one," he said, "and get the Maury County Sheriff on his way. Tell him 'shots fired,' okay?"

I nodded, his old face beginning to blur.

Granddad arched his neck, looking up, trying to take a breath. He looked at me; his hand fell on my hand, and he squeezed it. "Two," he said, his voice a rattle, his glance flashing to the .44. "Your training is complete, son," he whispered. He took his last inward breath, and with its exhalation he rasped, "Now, Mr. Green, defend our house." Then he was gone.

The last thing I felt able to do was to leave him there.

But this was a choice that, as far as I could tell, made itself. So I got to my feet.

The gun.

Hammer still cocked.

In my hand.

Checking the hallway: nobody.

I tiptoed quickly to his bedroom.

The nightstand again, this time to the phone on top.

Nine. One. One. Ringing.

Ringing again.

"Sheriff's office, what's your emergency?"

My lips moved in cold summary: "Shots fired at the Forty. Malachi Green is dead." I took a few ragged breaths as some grown-up words came pouring through from the other end of the line. I went on. "There's an intruder in our house. Send the sheriff." I didn't hang up; I set the handset down on the bed, and it sank into the still-warm ripples that had been made by my grandfather as he shoved his covers aside and leaped from his bed to rescue me not two minutes ago.

I moved out of his bedroom and down the hall.

As I passed by the door to my bedroom, I averted my gaze, sighting along the barrel of the revolver toward the stairs. I was past the point of no return.

Something went bust inside me, and I felt anger coming up from the ground. It surged through me, and I drew a deep breath, the words I wanted to use bubbling up and forming a dangerous cluster: "Leonard!" I screamed as loud as I could. "You either get out now or I kill you!"

Silence.

I was a young man ready to die, ready to kill, whichever was my destiny. *When these things are true, whom shall I fear?*

Then, coming from the living room downstairs: shards of laughter and a wicked song: "I got me Granddaddy's shotgun."

Chapter 44

Jon

He had found the twelve-gauge leaning up against the fireplace.

"Damn," I whispered.

Yeah, well, I argued inside, *I have right on my side. And Dirty Harry.* But these brave declarations were carried off as mere sentiment under the pressure of my just rebellion.

It was 1777, General Washington had been shot from his white horse, and independence now depended on me: a simple messenger boy. King George the Wicked and Insane roamed below unchecked.

I drew in a long breath as I paused at the top of the stairs and let it out. Tears smeared my vision. "Why won't you just leave me alone?"

"Because you're mine," came the coughing reply, and it could have come from anywhere.

I began my descent. "Not anymore." I was ready to kill again. To defend our house. The house of Malachi Green. A place where I belonged.

One stair at a time. Dead quiet. But halfway down, the wall on my left became an open railing: I'd be exposed. I needed a solution for this problem.

One more step.

The .44 magnum was heavy; it wrung the sweat out of my hands.

But it was powerful. I remembered what it had done to the milk jug.

Silently, while sighting down the barrel, I rotated to my left until the revolver's muzzle was aimed downward at the wall. The living room would be there on the other side of these thin sails of plaster.

I closed my eyes.

Slow, steady squeeze.

I saw the fireball through my eyelids, and the sound of the explosion was like God's own footstep. But I didn't have time to recover—the whole point was to give myself half a chance of making it down the stairs. So I shook my head and hustled, ears ringing as I came down two steps at a time onto the main floor, across the hardwood landing, bare feet feeling the cold linoleum of the kitchen.

Safe.

But for how long?

The kitchen window was wide open, and the screen had been torn off. *That's how he'd come in.* I growled at that, finding my holy fury once again.

I crouched low and cocked the hammer.

My ears were unwell. The ringing was getting worse, but I could hear the Leonard raging one room over. I knew this sound well.

I wondered if I might have hurt him.

I didn't have to wonder long.

The floor trembled with his approach. I knew what was coming. I scrambled under the table, turned, and raised the muzzle of my mighty cannon toward the corner of the wall where his head would appear.

Trembling. "No more," I whispered. I breathed. In. Out. Slow, steady squeeze. And as that wicked face centered itself to the full in my sights— I fired.

The .44 roared like a lion.

The Leonard went down in a hail of flame and lead and power and dust and blood.

Those black eyes would never again rain down fear upon me.

It was finally over.

Was I now free?

Chapter 45

Jon

The aftermath loosed in me a great well of sadness, and I drew from the flood of its overflow until the fire of my pain was quenched.

Then a new fire arose, and I was angry at Granddad for dying. I was angry with me for everything. And I was angry at the Leonard for everything else.

But more time passed.

Loss then became an even tide, the flood at length receding.

And I began to hear the echo.

I found memory to be a powerful force. A foolish part of me wished I had more memories with Granddad in them. But the wiser part—the Green one—understood that rare things were highly prized.

There was indeed an echo all around the Forty. In it were the memories I treasured. It was subtle; I had to listen for it. On quiet days when the sun drooped low over the meadow and night began to steal in, I could hear my granddad's stories coming back to me.

Oh, they were the same old stories alright, about the '39, and the Mud Cub, and most of all Alice.

But they said something different, something new every time.

I tried to catch the echo as it faded. Each time, it outran me. But each time, I had faith it would come again.

Chapter 46

Jon

Late fall, 1989. Just over two years later.

Mr. Jon Green, high school grad at fourteen. Well, fifteen, technically.

I didn't become a man at twelve years old. That was merely the night I took another man's life in self-defense. Lots of people, when they heard my story, assumed that was the moment manhood got its spark in me. That assumption was an obvious thing for almost anyone to think, but it was too obvious. Manhood couldn't be built on murder. Not while good men remained and abided.

No, I became a man sometime around the moment Granddad gave me the letter and snapped the photo—the one that showed us standing on the front porch.

Our own Model T.

And in truth, even before then.

I was awakening to the idea that it was a process, that it came in waves. I highly prized this revelation because most men were not men at all. They either slept their lives through—never activating, never catching fire—or they wasted along selfish and dead, as wraiths.

My life now was, in one way of eternal millions, a mystery to be solved. "It's not that the Good Lord is cruel; He just enjoys a good adventure," Granddad would have said. In other words, it depended how you saw things.

And because we saw things the way we did, the Green family carried on. Because there is always hope.

The sheriff never found the woman who was with the Leonard, whoever she was. She had most likely parked down the road and bugged out when she heard sirens. There had been plenty of those that night.

The sheriff had found me on the floor in the living room. I was by Granddad's chair, quaking, the revolver in my lap. Some of it was relief, some of it was because my body was burning off huge amounts of adrenaline, and some of it was because I had just survived my first gunfight at twelve years old.

There were two dead bodies in the house with me. One of them had belonged to my father, a man I love: Malachi Green.

Momma was hysterical about everything—I saw that coming from miles away—but by the time she got to the Forty late that night, she didn't allow me to see much of her worry.

Being a Green, that wasn't surprising.

From then on, she didn't look at me like I was a kid. She looked at me with a mixture of, *What's he gonna do next,* and, *I'm impressed.* I guess that meant I was on my way.

We (she and I) moved permanently to the Forty that summer. My beloved Tennessee hills.

The dog—we put her up for adoption at the pound before we left Chicago. Granddad wouldn't have wanted an animal in the house.

And besides, we didn't need a dog. There was more than enough to do at the Forty without a soft, citified dog complicating everything.

Momma had to hire a safe cracker all the way from Nashville to find out what Granddad's documents said. She said he'd taken out a million-dollar life insurance policy on himself, and there were other lawyerly details I didn't care much about at fourteen years old.

The date on the policy led me to believe it was one of the things he'd taken care of when he went to Columbia to get my name changed. It was one of his final acts.

But the insurance was only part of it.

In his will, he left the Forty to me. It was to be administered by Momma until I turned eighteen, when it would be 'mine-all-mine,' as he would have said.

Part of the will read this way:

> *Jon Green, I want you to read the book of Proverbs. A lot. It's in the middle; you can't miss it.*
>
> *Sarah, you come on home, lovely. You can live at the Forty as long as you promise you'll stop being a damn fool chasing career and instead*

As for the '39, the will stated, "If Jon's feet can reach the pedals," I had to drive it at least once a week, only in dry weather, and I could never sell it. Alice's Cadillac had to stay in the family.

Perfect.

The attorney who read the will asked me if I understood what the following sentence meant: "Jon Green, if you have a son one day, you will tell him Mud Cub stories." I smiled and told the man I understood perfectly well.

Our lives became quiet—front porch in the breeze with a good book under the shade of the sycamore quiet.

And this quiet was in possession of the full knowledge that somewhere up in that great sycamore out front there lay embedded deep in the soft wood at least a few balls of buckshot. My granddad had put them there right and proper, and that squirrel was damn lucky.

Meanwhile, there were hens and the sow to feed, there was fence to mend, and there was a goat to milk.

These things suited me.

I figured maybe one day I'd meet my best friend, and maybe she wouldn't live far from here. And she'd be the most beautiful woman in the whole wide world.

Kind of like Helen of Troy.

Kind of like Alice Benjamin.

THE END